River's bro[...]p and down i[...]t's fine. I get it. You're not interested."

But Edith was. She was more interested than she'd ever been before. But she couldn't admit that now. He might reach for her again. He might kiss her.

Then she opened her mouth because she wanted him to touch her, to kiss her...

But he reached for a broom instead and began sweeping up the shards of the vase she'd dropped. "You seem a little rattled," he remarked. "Had you been hearing anything else before I showed up?"

"What do you mean?" she asked.

"Any of those weird noises again?" he asked. "Like the clanging or the footsteps on the stairs?"

She shook her head. She almost wished she would have; it would have distracted her from thinking about him, from obsessing about him, about how passionately he'd kissed her, about how he'd carried her up those stairs...

* * *

The Coltons of Shadow Creek:
Only family can keep you safe...

THE COLTON MARINE

BY
LISA CHILDS

MILLS & BOON

First Published in Great Britain 2017
By Mills & Boon, an imprint of HarperCollins*Publishers*
1 London Bridge Street, London, SE1 9GF

© 2017 Harlequin Books S.A.

Special thanks and acknowledgement are given to Lisa Childs for her contribution to *The Coltons of Shadow Creek* series.

ISBN: 978-0-263-93042-9

18-0717

Our policy is to use papers that are natural, renewable and recyclable products and made from wood grown in sustainable forests.The logging and manufacturing processes conform to the legal environmental regulations of the country of origin.

Printed and bound in Spain
by CPI, Barcelona

Ever since **Lisa Childs** read her first romance novel (a Mills & Boon story, of course) at age eleven, all she wanted was to be a romance writer. With over forty novels published with Mills & Boon, Lisa is living her dream. She is an award-winning, bestselling romance author. Lisa loves to hear from readers, who can contact her on Facebook, through her website, www.lisachilds.com, or her snail-mail address, PO Box 139, Marne, MI 49435, USA.

A special thank-you to Melissa Jeglinski
for being a fabulous agent and friend.

Chapter 1

The darkness was all-encompassing. All-concealing.
Night was the only time River liked to come out now—
like the other nocturnal creatures that rustled around
in the brush. The noises made his horse uneasy, and it
shifted beneath him.

"It's okay, Shadow." He soothed the skittish stallion
with a pat along his silky mane.

Maybe he should have chosen another horse from
Mac's barn—one less temperamental. But there was
something about the formerly mistreated horse with
which River identified. Not that he had been mistreated. Physically. His mother wouldn't have wanted
to leave any signs of abuse on him or his siblings;
then she might have missed a photo op. Because she'd
been busy with ventures other than parenting, she had
missed pretty much everything else, though.

Of course she hadn't had a choice the past ten years; until her recent breakout, she'd been in prison. For— among those other ventures—murder. The man he'd believed was his father would have been a killer, too, had any of his attempts proved successful. He had just pled guilty to several counts of attempted murder and assault.

River should have been relieved the DNA test had confirmed that Wes Kingston wasn't actually his father. He'd never had much of a relationship with the man, anyway. Just like all his other half siblings, River used his mother's maiden name: Colton.

But even though he had never used it, there had been some comfort in knowing he was a Kingston. Now he didn't know who his father was or who he was, either.

But that wasn't just because of his paternity.

Despite the warm July night, he shivered and tugged his hat down lower over his face. Hopefully nobody else was out this late. But since his mother's prison break, there was always someone watching him and his siblings. The FBI, the police and of course the damn reporters—the ones from the national tabloids and that relentless website, *Everything's Blogger in Texas*.

River shouldn't have come back to Shadow Creek. Hell, he wouldn't have—had he had any other choice. As his fingers slid away from the brim of his Stetson, they brushed down the right side of his face over the strings holding the patch in place over his eye—his empty eye socket, actually—and along the ridge of the not-quite-healed scar on his cheek and jaw.

Now he couldn't leave Shadow Creek, and not just because he was still healing but also because of his siblings. He'd already been gone for most of the past ten years—leaving them alone to deal with the fallout of their mother's trial. Since he'd joined the Marines, no one else had accused him of being a coward.

But he knew...

And it didn't matter how many medals he had; he still considered himself a coward. He could have stayed and helped Mac with his younger siblings, could have worked the ranch with him.

He had been doing that since he'd come back. He'd started helping out while Mac's son, Thorne, who was also one of River's half siblings, was gone on his honeymoon. But Thorne and his new wife, Maggie, were back now, working on their house on the property, and River had stayed. It was too late now, though. He couldn't change the past.

Hell, he didn't even know his past anymore.

Who the hell was he?

Wes Kingston had no idea. Probably only one person knew for certain, and the police, the FBI and even the reporters hadn't been able to find her yet.

Livia...

There had been sightings of her in Florida. But Florida in July?

He snorted, and the horse echoed the sound. Livia hadn't liked the heat of Texas in the summer; there was no way she was in Florida now with the humidity and the bugs. So where was she?

For everyone else's sake, he hoped far away. For his...

Hell, it wouldn't matter if he found her. She wasn't likely to tell him the truth. But maybe she'd written it down somewhere.

If she had, the records or journals would be hidden somewhere on the estate, at La Bonne Vie, which in French translated to The Good Life. But life there hadn't been good.

The house, the acreage and the parties—it had all just been for show. A pretense. A lie. Like River's entire life. He needed to know what the truth was. But time was running out. After sitting vacant for ten years, the estate had finally been sold.

River doubted the new owner would let him search the place, especially after all the damage the FBI had done when they'd torn the place apart ten years ago looking for more evidence against Livia.

As if they hadn't already had enough. They'd searched it again after Livia's escape. But River didn't think they'd found what he was looking for. They didn't know the house like he did. They didn't know all of La Bonne Vie's secrets.

Neither did he, but he was determined to discover them. He squeezed his legs, prodding the stallion with his knees so it hurried forward along the trail that led from Mac's ranch to La Bonne Vie.

The horse felt his urgency and quickened his pace. River wasn't certain how long he had before the new owner either took up residency or tore down the place. Nobody knew who'd bought it or why.

The stallion bounded easily up the hill toward the expansive shadow sitting atop it. This was it—the house. It was some French-country monstrosity with seven bedrooms and eight bathrooms and countless fireplaces—not that it often got cold enough for a fire. Just like the house, the hearths had mostly been for show.

He and Shadow had already vaulted the fence between Mac's place and the estate. Then they'd wound around the base of the hill to head up the long circular drive. They now passed the fountain that gurgled in front of the house. If not for the property having a natural spring, the water probably would have stopped flowing years ago.

He tugged lightly on the reins, drawing Shadow to a stop next to that fountain. After sliding off, he tethered the horse to one of the gargoyles sitting on the edge of the fountain. The horse could drink while River found a way into the darkened house.

As he neared the front entrance, his steps slowed, his boot heels scraping across the surface of the brick pavers. This wasn't a good idea for so many reasons.

First off, he was trespassing.

Second, he might not like what he found.

And third, he might not be alone—because the moon glinted off the metal and glass of the car parked on the other side of the fountain. He cursed. But just as he cursed, he heard the scream.

So did the horse. Shadow rose up with an anxious whinny and tugged his reins free of the gargoyle. He took off toward Mac's ranch.

But River turned back toward the house. He wasn't the coward he'd been at eighteen. He didn't run from trouble anymore. Instead, he usually ran right into it. The last time he'd done that, though, he'd lost his eye and damn near his life.

What would he lose this time?

She had lost it. Edith Beaulieu was not the type of woman to scream like a banshee. She wasn't the type to scream at all. Not even as a child. But the dark house and all of its creepy sounds had unnerved her.

She'd called the power company days ago to have the service restored after ten years of the estate sitting empty. They'd assured her that it would be done. But when she'd stepped into the foyer and flipped on the switch, nothing had happened. The elaborate chandelier remained dark, its crystals reflecting only the faint light of stars shining through the tall windows and the light of her cell phone.

Of course, after ten years, the bulbs might have burned out. She had already considered that, so she'd brought a lamp with her. When she'd plugged it into a socket, though, nothing had happened.

Maybe the power company hadn't been able to get inside and throw the breakers? That was why she'd used her phone light to move throughout the house and try to find the door to the basement. Electrical boxes were usually in the basement. Even with the light from her phone, she stumbled over broken furniture and discarded drawers and papers. And other things that indicated animals may have taken up residence when the humans had left.

So she hadn't been too concerned about those first scurrying sounds she'd heard. She'd just shuddered at the thought of crossing paths with rodents or spiders or snakes. But when she'd finally found the door to the basement inside the kitchen, she'd heard something else—something that had sounded like footsteps—human footsteps—moving down the steps. And when she'd opened that door, the light of her phone had glinted off a pair of eyes at the bottom of those stairs.

That was when she'd screamed. Nobody else was

supposed to be inside this house—nobody but her. But when she looked again, she saw nothing. Had she imagined it? Had it been a person or an animal?

She couldn't be sure. All she'd seen was darkness but for the glint of those eyes. She shuddered as her heart continued to race. But she heard nothing now—no movement at all. Her screaming had probably scared away whatever it had been.

Torn between running for her car and going down to investigate, she hesitated at the top of the stairs. In the horror movies, the one who investigated always got killed. But then, so did the one who ran for her car. She drew in a deep breath, but it did nothing to calm her. Reaching inside her purse and pulling out her can of pepper spray made her feel a little better.

If Edith Beaulieu was going out, it was only going to happen after one hell of a fight.

She gripped the can tightly in one hand while she held up her cell phone with the other. The light illuminated the steps before her but could not penetrate the rest of the darkness of the basement. Her legs trembled slightly as she began the descent. Despite the heat of the July night, it was cold down there. The damp air instantly chilled her. Goose bumps rose along her usually smooth, dark skin. She had Mama to thank for her complexion; fortunately, that was all Edith had inherited from Merrilee MacKenzie Beaulieu.

Not the illness…

Unless she'd only imagined those eyes in the dark and had screamed for no reason. She shivered again, and it had nothing to do with the cold. As she reached the last step, she shone her light around the darkness, but it glinted off nothing now but boxes and crates and stacks of chairs and other furniture. She moved around the clutter toward a door off the hallway. As she pushed it open, the hinges screeched in protest. And above her the house creaked.

Since she'd unlocked the front door and stepped inside, she'd had a creepy sensation that she was not alone. First those eyes and now the noise against the floorboards—that sounded suspiciously like footsteps—confirmed it. Someone else was inside the house. But how had he or she gotten from the basement to the upstairs without passing her on the steps?

Unless there was another stairwell somewhere…

She'd heard the house had secret rooms. What about secret passageways?

She shivered again. But she wasn't really cold—not with how quickly her blood was pumping through her veins. She was scared. Her hands trembled so much that she nearly dropped the pepper spray canister and the cell phone, making the light bounce around the room. It glanced off the furnace, a couple of water heaters and a metal box on the wall. She'd found the utility room.

She hurried over to the electrical panel and opened the door. Then she fumbled with the breakers, pushing them the opposite direction of where they'd been. They must have been off because a light from the dirty bulb swinging from the rafters in the ceiling came on.

She expelled a slight breath of relief. At least she had light now. But then her relief fled as she heard more creaks—of the basement door and then on each step leading down. She fumbled with her phone, shutting off the light. Then she reached for the chain hanging from that swinging bulb. She needed darkness so she could hide. But then she remembered she was the one with the right to be there. And she let the chain slip through her fingers while she tightened her grasp on the canister of pepper spray.

Whoever else was here was trespassing, which probably meant he was up to no good. Squatting? Stealing? Or using the abandoned house for other nefarious activities?

She wished now she had a gun. But the pepper spray would have to suffice. She clutched it tightly—pointing it out in front of herself. And she waited.

Within seconds the utility room door groaned as it was opened the rest of the way. A dark shadow filled the doorway. He was too far away for her to spray and hit him. So she lifted her cell phone light toward his face. The brim of a hat pulled low shadowed it, but still she saw the scars and the patch.

And she screamed again.

The pounding of hooves against the ground sent a cloud of dust rising up into the night sky and a chill of unease racing down Mac's spine. He had returned only minutes ago from a date with Evelyn. She made him feel like a teenager instead of fifty-six. But the smile she always put on his face had slipped away when he'd found his house dark. No lights shone in the apartment above the stables, either.

Where was River? His truck was parked near the stables. But he realized why when the horse came into view, froth trailing from his mouth down his mane. The stallion looked mad. Or terrified, its eyes wild as it reared up on his back legs and stabbed at the air with his front hooves.

What had that damn stallion done? Had it thrown off River somewhere in the darkness? That unpredictable horse. Mac wouldn't have had him but for Jade. She wanted to help the horse, but she couldn't have him at Hill Country Farms. He wasn't safe for kids to be around, and she had too many young visitors to her place. She worked with him here when she had the time. But she was busy rescuing other former racehorses.

And Jade was scared. Half the time her eyes looked as wild as the stallion's. Maybe that was why she was so determined to help him.

But what if he'd hurt River?

The ex-Marine was still healing from whatever tragedy had happened on his last deployment. He refused to talk about it. Mac could understand River not wanting to answer the reporters' intrusive questions about his scars, about his missing eye... But he hadn't told his family anything, either.

Ever since he'd come back to Shadow Creek, he had seemed so lost.

"River?" Mac called out. Was he lost now? Where was he?

Careful to avoid the hooves, Mac grabbed the reins of the rearing stallion and tugged until the horse dropped to all fours again. With his other hand, he patted the horse's sweaty neck. "Settle down," he murmured soothingly. "Shh..."

He whinnied and tossed his head, pulling on the reins Mac tightly clasped. But eventually he calmed enough that Mac could lead him to the barn. He pulled open the door and led Shadow to his stall. There were other horses in the barn—ones River could have, should have, saddled up for his night ride.

Why had he taken the damn temperamental stallion? What had he been thinking?

Mac unfastened the saddle from the stallion and carried it to the tack room. He didn't trust Shadow—either to be ridden or to lead him back to where he'd lost River. Where the hell was that? From the amount of sweat that had saturated Shadow's coat, Mac could tell he had been running for a while. So Mac doubted River was anywhere on the ranch. He was farther away than that. But not so far that he would have needed to take the truck instead of a horse. Because of its proximity, the logical place was La Bonne Vie.

But why would River have wanted to return to a place he hadn't been able to wait to leave ten years ago? What was his sudden interest in La Bonne Vie? And what had happened to him there that the horse had returned without him?

Chapter 2

He should have ducked and run away. But River wasn't the coward he'd once been. Apparently he wasn't that smart, either. The last thing he needed was a shot of pepper spray in his good eye. But instead of running away, he rushed forward and clasped the screaming woman's wrist. Careful not to hurt her, he raised her arm, so if she sprayed, it wouldn't hit him directly in the face.

She struggled against him, bringing her body flush against his. While she was slender, her breasts were full and lush against his chest. And she smelled so damn good...

Like sunshine and some flower he couldn't quite place.

"Let me go!" she demanded, her voice sharp despite its thick Southern drawl. She didn't sound like she was from Texas. She didn't smell like it, either.

"Let go of this damn can," River said. With his other hand, he pulled the pepper spray free of her grasp. But he didn't release his hold on her finely boned wrist, even as he lowered her arm. Her skin was so silky and her pulse pounded wildly beneath his fingertips.

She stopped struggling and stared up into his face. And he saw the recognition dawn in her brown eyes. It was better than the look of horror she'd had when she'd initially seen him. When would he get used to that—to that reaction when people first saw him?

No. They didn't see *him*. They saw only the injuries. The damage.

He was damaged—and not just physically. He released her and stepped back into the shadows outside the circle of light cast from the dim bulb, and he pulled his hat down lower over his face.

"You're a Colton," she said. "River?"

He nodded, not surprised she recognized him. Every local news broadcast included some kind of report about the Coltons of Shadow Creek—either a history lesson on their illustrious family or a recent Livia-on-the-lam sighting. But this woman looked vaguely familiar to him, as well.

Where had he seen her?

He should remember. She was such a beauty with her flawless dark skin and long, thick, black hair that she would definitely be unforgettable had they ever officially met.

"You don't own this place anymore," she told him.

"I never owned it," he said. And for the past ten years the FBI had had custody of it, having seized it and whatever other assets of Livia's they'd been able to find. Of course they hadn't found them all. She had too many hiding places—so many just inside this house. He glanced around the cement walls of the cellar, wondering what lurked behind the concrete.

"Do you own it now?" he asked. She looked young, though, so young that he wondered how she would have been able to afford it. Unless it hadn't gone for much at auction.

Who would want a house with such a notorious past?

"I am here at the new owner's behest," she said.

"You're not. You're trespassing."

He shook his head. "No. I was just out for a ride when I heard you. Why were you screaming?"

She shivered. It was chilly and damp in the basement and she wore only a tank top and some long gauzy skirt. But he didn't think she was shivering because she was cold. She was scared.

"I saw someone…something…" She narrowed her dark eyes and studied him with suspicion. "Was it you?"

He shook his head again. "I didn't come inside until I heard your first scream."

She continued to stare at him as if weighing his words for truth.

"It wasn't me you saw," he insisted. A frisson of uneasiness chased down his spine, but he resisted the urge to shiver, as well. He reached for his weapon—before he remembered he wasn't wearing a holster. He wasn't armed. He hadn't thought he would need to be when he came home. But he should have known he'd never really been safe here—not with a mother as mercurial as his.

He probably didn't need a gun, though. But then

he remembered the scream—her first one, which had been full of terror. She had seen something.

"I'll check it out," he told her as he turned toward the door. Before he could step through it, she closed her fingers around his arm.

"Wait!"

"What?" he asked. Maybe she just wanted him to leave. Maybe she didn't believe that he wasn't the someone or something who'd made her scream the first time.

"Be careful," she urged him with obvious concern for his safety.

He held up the can he'd taken from her. "I have this." He took her hand from his arm and pressed the canister into it. "On second thought, you keep it."

She glanced down at it. "But why?"

"In case we really aren't alone down here," he said. "If there is an intruder, you're going to need it." He would have told her to leave, but he didn't want her walking alone through the house or getting so far away from him that he couldn't protect her from any potential danger. If she stayed in the basement with him, he could get back to her quickly if someone else was in the house. And she had the pepper spray for protection, as well.

She shivered again. But she closed her fingers around the can and clasped it tightly. "What about you—what will you use for protection?"

Images flashed through his mind—images of when he'd had to improvise in order to protect himself and his unit during combat. He flinched at the memories before focusing on her.

"I'll be fine," he assured her. He closed his hand

over hers on the canister. "Don't hesitate. Next time someone comes through that door, you spray."

"But what if it's you?"

"Then aim for my right eye," he told her.

Her gaze moved toward his right eye—to the patch—and her lips parted on a gasp.

He turned away again then and stepped through the door before he was tempted to do something stupid— like kiss her. It was safer for him to take on an armed intruder in the dark than make a move on a woman armed with pepper spray.

Intruder?

Their voices emanated clearly from the speakers inside the hiding space, summoning anger from the person listening to them.

They were the intruders. Neither the woman nor the man had any business being inside La Bonne Vie. The man hadn't appreciated the house when he'd lived there. And the woman...the one who'd opened the base- ment door and screamed...

No matter who her boss was, she absolutely had no business being here.

What had she seen? Had the light on her phone il- luminated enough for her to make an identification? She hadn't told the man anything specific about what she'd seen. She'd been vague, but maybe that had been on purpose. She would be smart to not trust him.

Trusting anyone was a mistake—one the *listener* would not make again. Nobody and nothing could be trusted.

So what had the young woman seen?

Enough to get her killed?

Probably.

The risk was too great to let her live. Whoever she was, she would have to die—like so many others already had to keep the listener's secrets.

His remark had shocked her so much that Edith took a few seconds before remembering what else she'd learned from all the horror movies she had watched: people never go off separately. Once that happened, they were picked off one at a time. She hurried out of the utility room into the hall.

But River was gone.

Heat rushed to her face at how she'd screamed when she'd first seen him. He'd probably thought it was because of the scars and the patch. But it was because he was so big and muscular and handsome despite the scars. Her pulse had continued to race, even after she'd recognized him. The news mentioned him often when reporting about his missing mother. He was the Marine who'd just recently returned—wounded—from his last deployment.

The media speculated that he must have been involved in an explosion of some kind. Nobody had confirmed that speculation, though. The government wasn't talking and neither was River Colton. But it was clear he'd been hurt. The scars on his face were still healing. And his right eye…

It was gone.

So it couldn't have been River whom she'd seen at the bottom of the steps when she'd first opened the door to the basement. Edith had seen a *pair* of eyes, both glinting in the darkness.

Hadn't she?

Or had she imagined it all like Mama used to imagine things—like Papa, long after he'd died?

Edith didn't believe in ghosts. Whatever her mother had seen hadn't been real.

What about what she'd seen?

What the hell had it been?

Despite the couple of lightbulbs that burned now in the basement corridor, the shadows were thick yet and still too dark to determine what each was. Edith wasn't going to try to figure it out at the moment. She'd found what she'd been looking for in the basement—the electrical panel.

Since she'd flipped the breakers, she had no reason to return to the utility room, where River had told her to wait for him. She had no reason to linger in the basement at all. She headed toward the stairs leading back up to the kitchen.

River Colton could find her when he was done searching the cellar. Edith was not going to try to find him. She shuddered as she remembered how a hapless female character always found her boyfriend in the horror movie—bludgeoned or chopped up or...

Not that River was her boyfriend.

Nobody was her boyfriend. She hadn't had one for a while. She didn't have any time for dating. She was too busy with her job. And from what she'd seen of the house in the dark, she knew she was going to be even busier getting this place ready for her boss.

As she headed up the steps, she noticed the door at the top was closed. River must have shut it behind himself when he'd come down to investigate after hearing her scream. She wished he had left it open; then she would be able to see if any lights had come on upstairs when she'd flipped all the breakers.

Nerves fluttered in her stomach at the thought of moving again through that mess of a mansion with only the faint light of her phone. She peered beneath the door but could see only darkness.

The lamp she'd plugged in must not have cast a glow wide enough to be seen in the kitchen. And none of the lights in the kitchen must have come on. She glanced down at her phone. Fortunately, the battery had enough charge left that she wouldn't lose that light. But she probably should have waited until morning to come out to La Bonne Vie.

She would have—had her uncle been home when she'd stopped by his ranch. But when she'd seen his truck was gone, she had driven over here. It was just next door. So she'd thought she might as well check to see if the power had been turned on as she'd requested.

She should have waited until morning, though. Then she wouldn't feel as though she'd stepped into one of those movies she had watched so often as a kid, trying to act tough in front of the others in her foster home. She hadn't just been acting, though.

She *was* tough. And independent and brave, she reminded herself as she reached for the handle of the door. But before she could close her fingers around the knob, it turned and the door opened.

A dark shadow loomed in the doorway above her. There was a light burning in the house behind him, but the dim glow only cast his face more in shadows as his wide shoulders filled the doorway.

Remembering River's advice to use the pepper spray next time, she fumbled with the canister, but it slipped through her grasp and tumbled down the steps. Then she lost her footing, as well. Arms swinging, she began to fall backward just as that shadow reached toward her.

She must have screamed herself out earlier because even though she opened her mouth, no sound emanated from her hoarse throat. She could only gasp as she fell.

Chapter 3

From the bottom of the stairs, River saw it happening—saw her falling. He saw the dark shadow at the top of the stairs, saw it reaching for her. Or pushing her?

He rushed forward, but before he could catch her, the woman's hand closed around the railing and she steadied herself. But he wrapped his arm around her small waist and pulled her aside, stepping between her and that threatening shadow.

She clutched at him as she tried to find her footing on the steps again. She wasn't going to fall, though. He had her in his one arm while he swung his other toward that shadow.

Just before his fist connected, the other man stepped into the light. And River jerked his arm back, exclaiming, "Mac! What the hell are you doing here?"

"Looking for you," Mac replied. "That damn horse

came back without you. I thought it threw you. That
you might be hurt." His dark gaze skimmed over River.
"But you look fine. What are you doing here?"

"I was out riding—"

"Not you," Mac said. He gestured behind River.
"What are you doing here, Edith? When I was looking for him, I noticed your car parked out front by the
fountain."

The woman tugged free of River's grip and leaned
around him. "Hi, Uncle Mac."

And now River realized why she looked so familiar.
He'd seen pictures of her in Mac's house. Of course,
she'd been younger then—much younger. Just a little
girl with thick braids and her front teeth missing. She'd
certainly grown up since those old photos.

She must have been at Thorne's wedding, though,
since they were cousins. River had made himself scarce
at the ceremony. He hadn't stood in the receiving line,
and he'd skipped the reception. He hadn't wanted to
draw any attention away from the bride and groom.
And since he'd been back, people tended to stare at
him. And ask intrusive questions about what had happened.

He didn't want to think about what had happened,
let alone talk about it.

"What are you doing here?" Mac asked his niece
again.

"I—I stopped by the ranch earlier," Edith replied.
"But you weren't there."

"I was out with Evelyn," Mac said. "But that doesn't
answer my question. What are you doing here—at La
Bonne Vie?"

"You don't know?" River asked. He knew Mac

wasn't particularly close to his niece; he had lost touch with her for years and felt bad about it. But River thought they'd reconnected during those ten years he'd been gone. Mac had written about her in some of the letters he'd sent River.

"No," Mac said, and a muscle twitched along his tightly clenched jaw. "Edith, what are you doing here?"

"I told you I'm moving out of New Orleans, that I'm moving to Texas."

"Yes," he agreed. "But you didn't tell me you were going to move *here*, to La Bonne Vie."

She shook her head, and her long hair bounced around her bare shoulders. She stood so close to River on the stairs that a few tendrils brushed across his cheek. It was so soft—so silky. "I'm not going to stay here. Not for long, anyway, just until…"

"Until what?" Mac asked. "What business do you have with La Bonne Vie?"

River turned toward her now, studying her beautiful face as she stared up at her uncle. "The business I work for—it bought the estate. My job is to get it ready."

"Ready for what?" Mac asked. "Ready for who? I don't even know who you work for."

Hearing the pain in the other man's voice, River turned toward him now. He felt as if he were intruding on a family moment. He'd often felt like that in his own home, though. In this home. But it had never really felt like home. Not when he'd been growing up here and certainly not now.

"This isn't the time or the place to discuss this," Edith said, and there was a coolness in her voice now that was nearly as chilly as the damp air in the basement.

"Why not?" Mac asked. "Your *company* owns this place now, right?"

"The company I work for," Edith said. "Not me."

"We're trespassing," River said. "At least that's what she told me when I came inside here to see why she was screaming."

Mac hurried down a few steps and reached out toward his niece, like he had been earlier. "You were screaming? Why? What happened?"

She shook her head. "It was nothing..."

"She spooked my horse," River said.

"I—I thought I saw something—someone inside." Her fingers skimmed over River's arm. "Did you find anyone? Anything?"

He shook his head. Of course he hadn't had time to do a thorough search. He'd heard the footsteps overhead—had heard the basement door creak open, and he'd rushed back to make sure she was safe, just as she'd been about to fall. "I didn't see anything. But even with the power on, most of the lights are out down here. I couldn't search thoroughly tonight. I can come back in the morning."

"You're not staying here," Mac told Edith.

"Of course not," she agreed. "I have a room booked at the local B and B."

"Why?" Mac asked. "Why would you stay there and not with me?"

She uttered a soft sigh that River felt brush across his cheek. "I didn't want to invite myself."

"You're family." Mac turned around and headed up the stairs. "Come on, you two, let's head back to the ranch."

Edith clutched River's arm now, tugging him back around to her. "You're staying there?"

He'd had no place else to go.

"Of course," Mac answered for him before he had the chance. "He's family, too." Only Thorne was his son. But Mac was the only father figure any of the Coltons had ever really known. Even before finding out Wes Kingston wasn't his dad, River had never been close to the man—not like he was with Mac.

But Mac wasn't really his father. He needed to find out who was. If the secret was anywhere, it was probably inside this house—in one of Livia's hidden lairs.

"Why don't you ride back with Edith," River suggested to Mac, "and I'll take another look around here before driving your truck back."

"You just said you can't search thoroughly until morning," Edith reminded him, and there was suspicion in her voice now, like she was beginning to question his motives.

He couldn't have that—not if he wanted to get back inside the house.

"You can ride with Mac in the truck," she said, "and I'll meet you both back at the ranch after I lock up."

"You're not staying here alone," River said.

"I told you I'm coming back to the ranch—"

"Something could happen to you while you're locking up," River pointed out. Something to make her scream again like she had—with such terror it echoed inside River's mind yet.

At the top of the steps, Mac turned back around and gestured for them to come up, too. "We're all leaving together."

Edith sighed, but she obeyed her uncle, heading up

the stairs ahead of River. He couldn't help but admire the sway of her hips beneath that long, gauzy skirt. And when she stepped into the material and nearly tumbled forward, he caught her around the tiny waist again and helped her up the rest of the way.

Her breath audibly caught and she pulled away from him as she reached the top. He couldn't blame her. With the way he looked, he could understand why she wouldn't want him touching her.

"Sorry," he murmured. "I just didn't want you to fall." Not wanting to see her revulsion, he turned back toward the stairs. So he didn't see her face.

He only heard her murmur, "Thank you…"

But he did see something—maybe—at the bottom of the stairs. A glint in the darkness. Was that what she'd seen? What she'd thought might be human? He stepped closer and peered down, but the glint was gone.

And he couldn't be certain what he'd seen—if anything. Hell, since losing his right eye, he didn't quite trust his vision anymore.

"Come on, you two," Mac urged them. "Let's get the hell out of here and head back to the ranch." It was no secret that he'd always hated coming up to the main house when he'd worked for Livia. And she had probably actually had more respect and affection for Mac than she'd had for the other men in her life—hell, even her own sons.

Just before he pushed shut the basement door, River glanced down those stairs again. The glint was back. It could have been eyes. Or maybe something shiny gleaming in the darkness. He couldn't be certain.

But whatever it was unnerved him like it had Edith.

He barely suppressed a shudder. There was something else inside this house, something that felt almost sinister.

Mac glanced across the truck console at where River sat quietly in the passenger's seat. "Are you really okay?"

The wounded Marine had been quiet since he'd stepped out of the house. Not that that was unusual for River. He had always been a quiet kid. And since he'd been injured, he had become even more withdrawn.

River nodded, then snorted derisively. "Can't believe you thought that horse threw me."

"You haven't been on a horse in years," Mac reminded him. And he was still recovering from whatever had happened on that last deployment, but Mac didn't have to remind him of that. He doubted it was ever far from River's mind.

"Doesn't matter," River said. "I haven't forgotten what you taught me."

Mac had taught all the Colton kids to ride. River was nearly as good a rider as Thorne, who was probably second only to Jade.

"I wasn't questioning your abilities," Mac assured him. "It's that damn stallion. He's skittish and unpredictable."

"So is your niece."

Mac snorted now. "You don't know Edith." She was one of the strongest, most determined and driven women Mac had ever known. Not that he'd known her that long. Thanks to the nightmare that Livia Colton had made of his life, he'd lost track of his sister and his young niece. But that was his fault. He should have made time for Merrilee and Edith as well as Thorne and the other Colton kids. He'd always known his sister was fragile. He just hadn't realized how fragile, however. Edith was nothing like her mother. But he wasn't certain she knew that. While they had reconnected once she'd become an adult, she was still quite guarded with him. So guarded that he hadn't even known the company for which she worked had bought La Bonne Vie.

"No, I don't know Edith," River admitted as he turned in the passenger's seat and leaned slightly over the console. "Why don't I know her?"

"You've been gone for ten years," Mac said.

"But why don't I know her from before then?" he asked. "I remember the pictures you had of her as a little girl, but I don't remember her ever coming to visit. She's from Louisiana, right?"

Mac uttered a sigh, but it didn't ease any of the heaviness in his chest, any of the guilt. "Yeah, she grew up in New Orleans. I lost touch with my sister and her for a long time. I didn't know…"

"Didn't know what?" River asked.

"Didn't know my sister had lost her husband and that she'd been struggling…"

"Financially?" River prodded when he'd trailed off.

Emotion choked Mac, and he could only shake his head. Even now he couldn't talk about it—couldn't think about it without the guilt overwhelming him.

Was that why River couldn't talk about whatever had happened to him? Did he feel some form of guilt, as well—for surviving when others hadn't?

Mac was glad the ranch was close, because he pulled into the driveway behind Edith's car and cut the engine and the conversation.

But River wasn't fooled. "Guess I'm not the only one who has things he'd rather not talk about."

Mac sighed. "I can't change the past," he said. "So there's no point in discussing it."

"Exactly," River agreed.

But Mac wasn't as convinced that was true for River. Maybe he needed to talk about it, to work through it and get beyond it. Before he could suggest that, River opened the passenger door and slipped out. He didn't stop, either—he headed straight for the barn. Hopefully he didn't intend to take that damn horse out for another ride.

"Hey," he called after him. "Aren't you coming inside?"

River didn't even turn back—just shook his head and continued to walk away.

"Where's he going?" Edith asked as she stared after his broad back. "I thought he was staying with you."

"He's staying in the apartment in the barn," Mac said. "I tried to get him to stay in the house…"

"Why wouldn't he?"

Mac shrugged. "He said he might disturb me."

"How?" she asked.

Mac glanced down at his niece's face, her dark gaze locked yet on River. She seemed awfully fascinated with the ex-Marine. While Mac loved River like a son, he wasn't sure the man would be good for anyone right now. He'd been through so much and probably had more than physical wounds.

"I think it's the nightmares." Even with River in the barn, he heard him sometimes—heard the shouting. It sounded like he was trying to warn someone.

Edith shivered.

"Let's get inside," he said.

She turned toward him now and shook her head. "I really can't stay. I have that room in town—"

"It would make more sense for you to stay here," he said. "So you'll be close to the estate, if you really intend to go back there."

"I have to," she said. But she didn't sound particularly eager to return.

Mac couldn't blame her. He hated that house, most of all he hated the memories it held for him. But like he'd told River, he couldn't change the past, so there was no sense in dwelling on it. He slid his arm around her shoulders and steered her toward the front porch.

Before they reached the stairs, though, she pulled away from him. A pang struck his heart. Would she ever forgive him for not being there for her when she'd needed him? She'd claimed, when they'd reconnected a half a dozen years ago, that she harbored no resentment—that she understood. But was that how she really felt?

Then he understood why she'd pulled away when she reached inside her purse and pulled out a vibrating cell phone. At least he hoped that was the reason.

"I have to take this," she said, but yet she hesitated.

And he realized why—she didn't want him to overhear her call. Was it from a boyfriend?

Or her mysterious employer?

Mac swallowed a sigh of disappointment that he wouldn't find out—because he had to respect her privacy. But he was worried that the secrets Edith was keeping might put her in danger, especially if she insisted on going back to La Bonne Vie alone.

Edith waited until the front door closed behind her uncle before she called Declan back. He had only let the phone ring a few times before hanging up moments ago. That was the way he was—too busy to waste his time.

He'd even been like that when they were kids.

Of course he wouldn't want to talk to her if she was with someone, either. He was fanatical about maintaining his privacy—especially in Shadow Creek. He'd come to town once when she'd been visiting her uncle, but he'd declined meeting Mac. She suspected, though, that Mac wasn't whom he hadn't wanted to meet.

He answered on the first ring. "Hey, you alone now?"

"Yes…" But as she said it, she glanced around—making certain. She didn't feel alone; she hadn't since she'd stepped through the front door of La Bonne Vie.

"Good."

He was obviously alone, as well. She felt a pang of regret over that; her boss was usually alone. But he always claimed that was the way he wanted it. It must have been, because, with his good looks and money, he could have any woman he wanted. But like her, he was too busy for relationships and too smart to want one.

"When do you plan to go to the estate in the morning?" he asked.

"I already checked out the place tonight," Edith said.

"Of course you have," he murmured with satisfaction. "What's the situation?"

"The power has been turned on," Edith said. "But I almost wish it hadn't been."

"Why's that?" he asked.

"Because I can see how much work I have to do," she said. "The place is a mess, Declan. It's going to take major work if you want it to be inhabitable."

"All it takes to be inhabitable is power and running water," he said.

"You haven't seen this place," Edith said. He'd bought it sight unseen. And she couldn't imagine why.

Something sounding almost like a growl rattled the phone. "I will soon," he said, his voice gruff with frustration. "I'm going to clear my schedule..."

Which meant *she* would have to clear his schedule— in addition to all her other responsibilities as his executive assistant.

"...and visit in a few weeks," he continued. "You'll need to have a room ready for me then."

"At the local B and B?" He hadn't stayed in town last time he'd visited her. And of course he'd refused to stay with her at Mac's. Instead he'd made the six-hour drive between Shadow Creek and Lake Charles, Louisiana, twice in one day.

He chuckled and replied, "At La Bonne Vie, of course."

She shuddered at the thought of anyone staying there. Of course, she'd already told her uncle and River that she intended to. It made sense for her, though— since she had so much work to do there.

"You should have a room there, as well," he told her, "if there's as much to do as you say..."

She sighed. "I didn't have the chance to do much of an assessment yet. I could barely walk through the place."

"Sounds like inventory might take you a while."

He'd bought the estate with all its furnishings. Edith knew how much he'd bid for it, which she'd thought was high even before she had seen the place. But Declan hadn't built his business into the success that it was by paying too much for real estate.

"I'll get it done," she assured him.

"You always do," he said. "That's why I know I can count on you."

She smiled over his praise but was compelled to admit, "I might need to hire some help to get the house ready for anyone to stay there, though."

"Edith, you know I don't want anyone snooping around La Bonne Vie."

She flinched as she thought of River being inside, along with Mac. Declan wouldn't like that. But River had only been investigating her scream. Hadn't he?

"Not snooping," she said. "Working on the place. You know the house has been empty for ten years." Supposedly. It hadn't felt empty tonight, though—even before River Colton had showed up. "It needs to have things fixed I'm not qualified to repair—like the central air-conditioning unit and maybe the plumbing and probably some windows." Because the animals must have gotten into the house somehow.

Declan's sigh rattled the phone now. "Just make sure whoever you hire can be trusted. And that no one knows I bought the place."

She uttered a sigh now—of frustration. "Of course. I know my job."

To protect his privacy at all costs.

She glanced back at the house. Through the front window, she saw Uncle Mac moving around, getting his house ready for her. She hated not being able to tell him more about her life. He clearly thought she didn't want to include him in it. But she would—if she could.

"You had me sign a confidentiality agreement in

my employment contract," she reminded him. But that wasn't why she kept Declan's secrets.

"You know why I did that," he said. "It isn't easy for me to trust."

"I know."

"It's not easy for you, either," he said.

No. It wasn't.

And for some reason River Colton's face came to her mind. Even with that scar and patch, he was ridiculously handsome—not that she'd seen much of his face tonight with how low he'd pulled that hat.

But she remembered how he'd looked on news reports. His hair was thick and brown but always worn in a short, military-style cut. His eyes—eye—was a bright green, his gaze so piercing that it could nearly cut through a person. At least that was how he'd looked at the reporters and photographers bold enough to take his picture.

He hadn't quite met her gaze tonight—until that moment before he'd gone off to investigate. Then he'd looked at her and leaned close, close enough that for a moment she'd thought he'd been tempted to kiss her.

Or maybe she'd only imagined that, like she'd imagined seeing those eyes glinting at her from the darkness. At least she was going to convince herself of that, since she had to go back.

River had said he would go back with her in the morning to thoroughly check out the place. Had it just been coincidence, like he'd claimed, that he'd been out riding when he'd heard her scream?

Or did he have some other motive for showing up at La Bonne Vie tonight?

But River wasn't the only one she suspected wasn't being completely honest with her.

"What's your plan?" she asked her boss. "What do you intend to do with the estate?"

There was a long moment of silence—so long that she thought the call might have been lost—and then he replied, "I'm not sure…"

Neither was she. She wasn't certain he was telling the truth. But before she could pry any further, he clicked off the phone.

She gripped it tightly, tempted to toss it, before she calmed her frustration and slid it back into her purse. Despite the warm night air, a sudden chill swept through her—raising goose bumps on her skin.

She felt as if she was being watched. But when she glanced to the house, Uncle Mac was sitting with his back toward her. He wasn't watching her.

But someone was…

Chapter 4

The scene played out in slow motion—like it always did. He was just about to make the call—just about to send everyone in—when he felt it. The wrongness of it. The feeling was like a heavy rock lying low in his guts.

Something wasn't right.

But Henry jumped the gun and headed in—and as he did, he tripped the wire stretched across the entrance to the abandoned hotel. The blast knocked River back, lifting him off his feet. His shout rang out—too late— as he flew through the air with the dust, the debris, the shrapnel and the other bodies.

Before he hit the ground, though, someone caught him, wrapping slender arms around him, holding him down. That had happened that day, as well; someone had held him back from going in—from trying to find the others.

He'd fought that person. Today he didn't fight. Instead he jerked awake and stared into a pair of big eyes dark with concern.

"Are you okay?" Edith asked.

She was sitting on the edge of his bed, her arms wrapped around his bare chest. She was nearly bare, too, but for an exercise bra and brief shorts. Her skin was as slick with perspiration as his.

His heart had already been racing from the dream, now it beat even harder and faster as desire rushed through him. His throat thick with passion, he could only nod.

"I was just getting back from a morning run," she said, "and I heard you shouting."

He cleared his throat. "Dream—it was just a dream." And maybe so was this—her being here with her arms wrapped around him.

As if just realizing she held him, she jerked back. "I—I'm sorry," she said. "I shouldn't have…"

He released a ragged breath. "Guess we're even now," he said. "I rushed in last night when I heard you screaming and now…"

Had he been screaming? Sometimes, when he relived the explosion, he felt the pain all over again. Self-conscious now, he touched his face. At least he hadn't taken off the patch before he'd fallen asleep. But he had taken off his hat. With the sun shining through the bedroom window, his scars were clearly visible.

She wasn't staring at his scars, though. She wasn't even looking at his face. Her gaze was trained on his chest. The vest had protected that during the explosion. He had no scars beneath the dusting of dark hair.

Just his—and Henry's—dog tags dangled from around his neck.

Finally, she glanced up and met his gaze. "I'm—I'm sorry," she stammered again. "I just wanted to make sure you're all right."

"I'm fine," he assured her.

Now that she was looking at his face again, he could see the doubt in her beautiful dark eyes.

What the hell had she heard?

The heat that had rushed through his body with her touch spread up to his face now. He was embarrassed over her catching him in such a weak moment.

"When are you heading back to La Bonne Vie?" he asked.

She blinked, breaking their locked gazes. "Right after I shower."

New images flashed through his mind, of her standing naked beneath a spray of water. He groaned.

And she reached out but pulled her hand back just before it touched his face. "Are you sure you're okay?"

He nodded. He would have stood up, but the sheet tangled around his hips was all that hid his reaction to her closeness, to her touch. Even all sweaty from her run, she smelled like she had last night. Like fresh air and flowers...

"What is that smell?" he asked.

She stood up and stepped back, away from his bed. Then she touched her own face now and wiped away some of the perspiration. "I was running—"

"Not that," he said, although even her sweat smelled sweet. "The flowers. What kind of flowers do I smell every time I'm near you?"

"Gardenias," she replied as she backed toward the door to the stairwell that led to the stables below.

"Gardenias," he repeated as she slipped through that doorway. He smiled as he heard how hard her shoes slapped against the steps.

She was running again—away from him.

But she hadn't looked horrified—like he'd thought she had been last night when she'd first seen him. Instead she'd seemed almost flustered, as if she'd been as affected by his nearness as he had been by hers.

He pushed his hand over his face, down over his scar. Hell, he must have still been dreaming. She couldn't have looked at him like he had imagined— like she was at all interested in him.

For one, just as she must have heard him shouting through the open window of the apartment, he had heard her through it, too—last night when she'd been talking to someone on her cell phone.

Her boss or her boyfriend?

The affection in her thick Southern drawl had been apparent, and he wouldn't have expected someone to have such an affinity for an employer. She had definitely been talking to whoever had bought La Bonne Vie, though. Apparently even she wondered why the man had purchased the estate. Along with the affection, River had also heard frustration in her voice. Whatever her relationship was with the caller, it was complicated.

So River doubted she had any interest in him. She had more than enough to handle already. And he knew he had no future with anyone until he'd retraced his past and discovered who he really was. Since Edith was distracted with her difficult job and her difficult boss, she might not notice his snooping around the estate.

His stomach muscles clenched with dread over the thought of going back to La Bonne Vie. But it was the only place that might hold the answer to who he really was.

Edith's skin was chilled—from the cold shower she'd taken. She had needed it to bring her to her senses, though. She couldn't believe she'd been ogling River Colton like she had. The man was wounded; he had very obviously been through hell. And she'd been attracted. Of course she had been concerned, too.

But then she'd noticed his body—his hard, muscular body. She had never seen so many sculpted muscles, his slick skin stretched taut over them. Her pulse quickened even now, thinking of them.

Or maybe her pulse was quickening because she was about to unlock the front door of La Bonne Vie. It shouldn't have been as scary now, in the bright light of morning, as it had been last night, cloaked in darkness and full of shadows.

But now she could see the neglect of the last ten years—in the paint peeling away from the door and the fascia and the window frames. Moss clung to the brick walls. The landscaping was overgrown, vines climbing up the lattice in the windows to cover them—like that black leather patch covered River's right eye. Trees overhung the roof, some big limbs even lying across it.

She'd told Declan it was going to be a big job to get the place ready. But even she had underestimated the amount of work it would take. She wasn't going to undo ten years of neglect in a few weeks' time. But Edith had never shied away from work before. She would get the job done—just like she'd told Declan she would, just like she always did.

Of course working as hard as she did left little time for anything else—like a personal life. Like friends. Like men…

She thought of only one man, though—of River Colton, his chest bare and heaving with his pants for breath. He was the last man with whom she could get involved even if she had time. He had issues she wasn't prepared to deal with again.

And she had La Bonne Vie.

She slid the key in the lock, but before she turned it, the knob turned—easily. The door hadn't been locked. But she was certain that she had the night before when they'd all left together.

Why wasn't it locked now?

"Damn this house…" She pushed open the door but hesitated before stepping inside the foyer. She reached into her purse instead, but her fingers fumbled across notebooks and pens, her wallet and plastic makeup containers. She couldn't find the hard metal of the pepper spray canister. Then she remembered she had dropped it last night. It was under the basement stairs.

"Not going to do me a whole hell of a lot of good down there," she murmured.

She peered around before stepping across the threshold. "Hello?" Her voice echoed throughout the two-story foyer—off the marble floor and the ornate plaster ceiling. The paint was peeling off the plaster like it was the exterior and several crystals in the chandelier were shattered, fragments lying on the scratched marble floor.

What were Declan's plans for the house? Did he want it restored?

From estimating previous projects, she had an idea how much money it would take to return the mansion to its former glory. More than Declan would probably be able to get out of it—if he intended to flip it, like he had other properties. He wasn't just CEO of SinCo; he'd built the company from the ground up. So maybe he was going to develop the land instead. The three hundred acres might get him a return on his initial investment if he turned it into a housing subdivision or something. But she grimaced at the thought of Uncle Mac's ranch adjoining a real estate development.

"Hello!" she called out again. Nobody else's voice echoed back at her. She heard nothing else. No creaking. No footsteps. Not even the scurry of rodent feet.

She shuddered at the thought of dealing with rats or mice. But no doubt animals had moved in when the humans had moved out. That was probably what she'd heard and seen the night before—some nocturnal creature like a raccoon or possum.

She probably hadn't actually locked the door last night, either. As rattled as she'd been, she might have turned the key the wrong way before pulling it out. Maybe instead of locking it, she had unlocked it.

She expelled a slight breath of relief at the rationalization. Of course she knew that was what she was doing—trying to convince herself that everything was fine. She had been doing that most of her life, so it was second nature to her now.

It was also how she had survived. So she wasn't about to change her ways. Even though she was only twenty-seven, she was still too set in them. Or maybe, as some people including Mac and Declan had accused her, she was too stubborn to change. Instead of being insulted, she'd always taken that as a compliment.

She was tenacious. As she glanced around the damaged house, she was glad that she was. A less tenacious woman might have turned around and walked back out.

As damaged as the house was, though, it was still apparent how beautiful it had once been. The foyer was quite grand, with French doors opening off it on the left to a parlor and living room and an arched hallway to the right leading to the dining room and kitchen. And in the middle of the space wound a grand staircase to the second-story landing.

She could almost hear the music from the parties she'd heard had been held here. The murmurs of conversation, the tinkling of laughter...

What had it been like to grow up here? It was a far cry from the overcrowded foster home where she and Declan had grown up. Was that why Declan had bought it? Did it represent some sort of accomplishment to him?

She knew it was important to him. She just didn't know why. But because it was important, she had to get it ready for him. He couldn't see it like this or he might be horribly disappointed—in the house and in her.

She turned around again, surveying the damage. "Where do I start?" she murmured.

The kitchen. She would need the plumbing and appliances functioning in order to stay there while she did inventory of the furnishings, and Declan would need it working for his visit, as well. La Bonne Vie was too far from town to order takeout. They would have to be able to prepare their own meals. When he came, he would have to tell her what he intended to do with the estate. Maybe he just hadn't said yet because he wanted to assess the property in person before he decided.

She passed through the dining room, with its elegant coffered ceiling, to the kitchen. Sunlight worked its way through the vines and grime covering the many windows to gleam off the stainless steel counters that looked like they had begun to rust. The wooden floor had buckled near where the sink must have leaked. The doors to that cabinet stood open, as if they'd rotted off their hinges. She could smell the dankness of water damage and mold.

She would need a plumber for certain and definitely a carpenter. She moved toward the stove, about to check the gas, when she heard the noises again. The basement steps creaked as if beneath someone's weight.

Instinctively she reached for her purse again, but then remembered the pepper spray was gone. So she reached instead for the metal pot holder dangling over the island, and she grabbed a heavy iron skillet. Declan had taught her how to swing a bat. She suspected this wouldn't be much different.

It would do for protection.

Drawing in a deep breath, she opened that basement door again. But she didn't see anything this time. Was it just the sounds of a neglected house settling into disrepair?

Something scraped across cement, and she knew it was more than the house. Something—or somebody—was down there. But she was the only one with a right to be in this house—in Declan's house.

So she started down the stairs with the frying pan held over her shoulder like a bat. She was ready to swing. But when she reached the bottom step, she couldn't tell where that scraping noise had come from.

It was farther away than the stairs, than the utility room. She had no idea how big the basement was or where the dark hallway might lead. She needed more than the frying pan. So she moved around the stairwell until she stood beneath it. Cobwebs brushed across her face and clung to her hair, but she felt around in the shadows until she found it—the can of pepper spray.

Its metal was dented and dirtied with dust. As she reached for it, she noticed a bright patch of color lying in the dirt next to it. She picked up the piece of pink lace along with the can. The handkerchief must not have rolled around in the dirt like the pepper spray because it wasn't nearly as dirty.

Where had it come from?

She doubted River had had it on him the night before. But Mac could have; it might belong to the woman he'd started dating, Evelyn. Edith had met her at Thorne's wedding. She dropped it into her purse so she could ask him about it later. But she held on to the pepper spray yet because she heard that noise again— that scraping noise...

Someone else was down here. This time Edith would find the intruder and deal with him once and for all.

Why had it taken ten years after seizing the estate for the FBI to sell it? Why now? For a decade, it had sat empty—abandoned.

Now there were too damn many people coming in and out, poking around.

Trembling fingers reached for the volume on the

speakers, turning them down. It wouldn't do for anyone to hear that echo—of that damn scraping noise.

What the hell was going on?

The person didn't tremble with fear but with rage. With fury.

Those shaking fingers reached for other things now—for the gun lying atop an old bureau. Or the knife…

Even from down here, in one of the secret rooms, someone might be able to hear a gunshot. And if they came to investigate…

He or she would have to die with whoever was investigating now. That scraping sound was against one of the walls of the secret room. Too close.

So close that whoever it was might accidentally trip the switch to open the door. And if they did that, they would have to die.

The person picked up the knife and gripped it tightly. Yes, it would have to be the knife.

It would be quick and quiet. And there were other rooms where a body could be hidden…where it might never be found.

Chapter 5

Excitement coursed through River. He was so glad he'd rushed over to the estate while Edith had been in the shower at Mac's, so he'd had time to investigate before she showed up. This had to be one of them—one of Livia's secret rooms. The wall wasn't thick enough to be an exterior one. It wouldn't have been installed to support anything, either. He'd found it at the back of the wine cellar. Maybe it was just a place to store more expensive bottles.

But Livia wouldn't have hidden those. If she had anything of value or beauty, she had put it on display. She'd only hidden her dirty money and her secrets and the evidence that had eventually put her away.

His paternity was one of those. Who was his father that Livia had hidden his identity? One of the drug dealers or human traffickers with whom she'd associated?

The thought turned River's stomach. He pulled the crowbar back from the wall. He'd been shoving its end between the bricks of the cement wall, trying to get them to budge. He hadn't wanted to knock them down; he suspected instead that one of the cracks between the blocks hid a lever—something that would open the entire wall.

He could see where the dust on the ground had been disturbed around it. Maybe the FBI had done it when they'd searched the house again. But that had been a few months ago, long enough for the dust to have settled again.

Unless it kept getting disturbed.

Edith might have seen something—someone—the night before. If she hadn't screamed...

If he hadn't rushed in when he had...

Would that person have done something to her? Hurt her?

His stomach flipped again at the thought of her being in danger or worse yet, hurt. He had to make certain that didn't happen. And the best way to do that would be to find that person wherever he was hiding.

Whatever he was hiding...

River had had enough of secrets. It was time to learn the truth—no matter how horrible that might be. He lifted the crowbar to the wall again. Just as he began to swing the tip toward what looked to be a bit of metal sticking out between the blocks, he heard it.

The scrape of shoes against the concrete and a soft gasp. He dropped the crowbar and whirled around to face Edith. She had her can of pepper spray grasped tightly in one hand and a frying pan in the other.

"Are you going to blind me or cook me?" he asked.

"You're lucky I didn't spray you or hit you," she said with a snort of disgust. "What the hell are you doing down here again?"

Feigning surprise, he lifted a brow. "I'm checking out the house like I told you I would last night."

"And I told you that wasn't necessary," she said.

"I promised Mac that I'd make sure you'd be safe here," he said, which wasn't exactly a lie. They'd all talked about his coming back the next morning to check the place out. "I wanted to make sure there really wasn't anyone else in here."

Her big, dark eyes narrowed as she studied his face. "Seems funny the only person I ever actually find inside is you. Why do you keep showing up here?"

If he told her the truth, that he was looking for information, she'd probably toss him out and never allow him back inside. So despite how much he hated them, he'd actually have to keep a secret of his own.

It wasn't the only one he was keeping, though. There were things that had happened while he'd been deployed that he couldn't talk about—even if he'd wanted to. He was honor bound to his country and his fellow soldiers. He wasn't honor bound to Edith.

Something else bound him to her, though—a desire that quickened his pulse and heated his blood every time he was near her. And he wasn't near enough. He stepped closer to her and lowered his voice as he finally answered her question. "You," he said. "You're the reason I keep showing up here."

Her full lips parted on a soft gasp, and her eyes widened again. "Are you flirting with me?" she asked.

Like her uncle, she was straightforward. He appreciated that. Hell, he appreciated entirely too much about her—like her body and her face and her voice and her sexy-as-sin scent.

He laughed and touched the scars on the right side of his face. "Like you'd be interested in me…"

She gasped again, but it was his name that slipped out between her lush lips. "River!"

"It's fine," he assured her. "I'm not looking for pity." That would be a hell of a lot easier to find, though. He'd just have to go into town or to a family function. They all looked at him like that.

"What are you looking for?" she asked.

And he tensed. She wasn't just straightforward. She was smart, too.

She gestured at the crowbar he'd dropped. "I heard you scraping at something."

He shrugged. "I was just killing some spiders."

Her eyes were still narrowed. "With a crowbar? What do you swat a fly with? A shovel?"

"The crowbar was handy," he said. "And the spiders were big."

She shuddered in revulsion. She wore more clothes than she had last night or this morning. Now she had on jeans and a long-sleeved T-shirt—probably because of the bugs and spiders she'd known would be in the house. She glanced around the basement. "That's all you found down here?"

"I found some rats and a squirrel." But he knew he'd been close to finding something else. If he'd hit that latch in the wall, he might have opened one of his mother's secret rooms. He might have found some of her secrets. "Oh, and a snake, too."

She shuddered again. "Let's go upstairs, then," she said. And she hurried down the hall toward the stairs.

He appreciated following her, appreciated the curve of her hips in her jeans, and appreciated how her butt moved as she climbed the steps. Her legs were long and toned—probably from the running. She was slender but not so slender that she didn't have lush curves.

When she reached the top, she glanced back at him—as if she'd been aware of his staring. As if she'd felt it.

He wanted to touch her, so badly that he curled his fingers into his palms. She was already leery of him. He had to be careful.

But he found himself admitting, "I am looking for something…"

She tensed now. "What?"

"A job," he said.

"I thought you've been working with Uncle Mac on the ranch," she said.

He nodded. "But like I told you, I'm not looking for pity. And I think that's the only reason he's made work for me. Thorne really runs the place. They don't need me."

That was true. They didn't. Nobody did. He'd been gone ten years and they'd all functioned just fine without him. He really had no reason to stay in Shadow Creek—except that he had no place else to go.

He wasn't about to feel sorry for himself, though. He hadn't lost nearly as much as some people had. "But I need to do something…" Like find out who the hell his father was. "And it looks like you need a lot done around here."

Her dark eyes widened, and she blinked her long, thick lashes. "You want to work here? For me?"

He nodded. "It would be the perfect solution to

both our problems. You need work done, and I need to work." That was true. If he didn't keep busy, he would have too much time to think—too much time to think about what he and the others on that last mission had lost.

She narrowed her eyes again and studied him with skepticism and suspicion. "How do I know you can handle the job?" she asked. Gesturing at the kitchen sink, she asked, "Have you done any carpentry work? Any plumbing?"

"I have," he said. "During high school, I worked summers for Rafferty Construction, and since I've been back, I've helped my sister-in-law Allison, who owns the company now, with some projects."

"Why aren't you working for her now?" she asked.

"Are you in Human Resources?" River asked. Because he felt like he was being interviewed. "What exactly is your job title?"

Her wide mouth curved into a slight, sexy smile. "Everything," she said. "That's my job title. So yeah, I've been part of the hiring process. My boss usually has to approve all hires, though."

"You don't think he would hire me?" River asked.

"He is very private," she said. "He doesn't want anyone to know he's purchased La Bonne Vie."

"Why not?"

Her smile slid away, and she looked tense.

And he realized she didn't know, either.

She shrugged. "That's his business. And he doesn't want anyone else knowing it."

"I can respect that," River said. "That's why I'm not working for Rafferty Construction. Coworkers stared, asked questions. And reporters were able to track me down on the jobsites. They took pictures…" He shuddered like she had over the spiders.

"You don't think they'll find you here?" she asked. Even as she asked it, they heard the rumble of engines as vehicles pulled into the driveway.

He groaned. "I hope they haven't. Maybe that's just Mac again." But he doubted it. Mac had trusted that River would make sure his niece was safe here. And he wasn't likely to willingly return to La Bonne Vie unless he had a damn good reason.

Maybe they'd caught Livia, and she was back behind bars where she belonged. But someone would have called him with that news. At least one of his siblings would realize he'd want to know. He pulled out his cell and stared down at the standard screen saver.

He had missed no calls.

And they wouldn't have driven out here. Nobody but Mac knew that he'd intended to come back to La Bonne Vie. And Mac thought he'd only been doing that to keep Edith safe. But if those were reporters pulling up outside the estate, who was going to keep him safe?

Edith hadn't missed the dread on River's face—the tension tightening his already clenched jaw. He didn't want to see if those were reporters who had pulled up outside. And she didn't blame him.

It wasn't his responsibility. "You can stay in here," she offered, as she walked down the hallway heading from the kitchen back to the foyer.

"You shouldn't go out there alone," he said as he followed her. It wasn't like when he'd followed her down the basement hallway. Then she'd felt his gaze on her— on her body. And her skin had heated.

He wasn't looking at her at all now. His neck was arched, as he tried to peer out the windows through all the ivy covering them.

She laughed off his concern. "I'm usually alone," she told him, "in far more dangerous situations than this."

He caught her arm and spun her back around in the foyer. "Why? Where?"

She laughed harder. "I grew up in New Orleans." But she'd thickened her drawl and pronounced it the correct way. "I'll be fine, *cher.*" She held up her hand with the canister of pepper spray in it. "I have this."

He tilted his head and studied her face. "Have you ever used it?" he asked.

Her lips curved down, her smile slipping away, as she remembered and nodded. It hadn't been pretty, but she had done what she'd had to do. She still felt bad about it, though.

"Good," he said. "Don't hesitate to use it again if you need to."

With him and his ridiculously muscular body beside her, she doubted she would need to use it. He would scare anyone away. But he stepped back as she opened the door, so whoever was outside would see only her.

Lightbulbs flashed, blinding her, as questions bombarded her. "Are you the new owner of La Bonne Vie?"

"What is your name?"

"What are your plans for the place?"

Squinting against the bursts of light and the sun shining overhead, she peered at a crowd of faces and microphones and cameras. And she understood why River had stepped away from the open door.

Growing up as one of the notorious Coltons, he'd

been hounded by paparazzi probably almost his whole life. Except for when he'd been deployed.

Reporters had speculated where he was those ten years he'd been gone. But none had known. She wondered if even his family knew.

"Miss, what is your name?"

"What do you do for a living?"

"Aren't you afraid of owning Livia Colton's home?"

Her hand clenched on the pepper spray canister. She was tempted to use it. Maybe this was how River had wanted her to. But she resisted the urge.

Instead she raised her voice and said, "You are all trespassing! Leave the estate immediately or I will call the police and report you."

"So you are the owner?" a male reporter persisted. But he sounded skeptical. "You have the authority to report trespassers?"

She groaned at the man's arrogance and chauvinism. "I have a legal right to be here," she said. "You do not."

But her threat hadn't compelled any of them to leave. They kept taking pictures and asking questions. And her head began to pound.

She'd worried about someone being inside the house earlier. But she'd had no idea how bad it was to have them outside. Yet that didn't seem to be enough for them. They crept closer to her and lifted their cameras to snap pictures over her head—of the interior.

"What is the condition of the home?" one asked.

"Is there any evidence of Livia's crime spree left inside?"

She pulled the door shut behind herself. "You need to leave. Now!" She reached for her purse, trying to fumble her cell phone from the inside of it. Her fingers skimmed across the bit of lace she'd picked up earlier. But she couldn't find her phone.

Had she dropped it somewhere? Left it on the kitchen counter?

Nobody listened to her. They stepped closer, as if they were going to reach around her to open the door. Was River still inside? Would he help her stop them?

She heard another vehicle pull in. Or were more of them going to just keep coming?

A horn blared, drawing the reporters' attention toward the big truck that had roared up the drive. "Get the hell out of here!" a deep voice boomed as Thorne Colton stepped out of the driver's door.

Edith breathed a sigh of relief at the sight of her cousin. He rushed up toward where she stood at the front door. As he moved through the crowd, they took his photo and bombarded him with questions.

"What are you doing here, Thorne? Do you have a relationship with the new owner?"

"Are you going to be living on the estate again?"

Thorne held up his big hands and waved the reporters off. "I've called the sheriff. He will be arriving soon to arrest anyone who is still trespassing on the property."

While they hadn't listened to Edith, they seemed to believe Thorne and started moving toward their vehicles. As they walked away, Thorne snapped a couple photos with his phone. "And if anyone comes back, these pictures will be turned over to the sheriff," he said. "So you will be arrested for illegally accessing a private property."

One bold reporter lingered and had the audacity to ask, "Aren't you trespassing, too?"

"Then I guess the sheriff will arrest me when he gets here, and we'll be going to jail together, Jake." His bluff was enough to send the reporter scurrying toward his network van.

Edith didn't relax or turn to her cousin until all the vehicles had driven off. Then she threw her arms around him and hugged him tightly. "Thank you!" She pulled back slightly. "And thank you for calling the sheriff!"

"I didn't," he replied. "He's worthless."

"Good to know…" What if there really had been an intruder in the house? If she had called for help, apparently none would have come.

But she hadn't had to call…because she had River. She'd *had* River. Where had he gone?

Only Thorne had come to her rescue this time. Why?

Her brow furrowed as she stared up at her cousin's handsome face. His skin was lighter than hers and his eyes a pale brown. Even though they were just cousins, they looked more alike than Thorne looked like his brother River or any of his other siblings for that matter. But no matter what they looked like, all the Coltons were attractive.

An image of River flashed into her mind again—shirtless as he'd been that morning with a couple sets of dog tags nestled against his pecs. Her face heated and she stepped back.

"How did you know I needed help?" she asked.

"River," Thorne replied. And he glanced around as if expecting his brother to be there.

Edith shrugged. "I don't know where he went." She hadn't even known how he'd gotten there. When she'd arrived, the only vehicle parked outside had been hers. She hadn't seen a horse, either—unless he'd put it inside the barn behind the house.

She sighed as she glanced toward the other structures on the property. She would have to inspect those buildings and inventory their contents, as well. She had a big job to do. Would it be more manageable with River's help? Or would he just prove a distraction she didn't need?

Thorne hadn't seen his cousin since his wedding and he hadn't had much of a chance to speak to her that day. There had been so many other guests but most of all there had been his bride, looking more beautiful than he'd ever seen her. And he hadn't been able to focus on anything but her and how much he loved her and the family they were about to start together. Maggie was already carrying his baby.

Guilt flashed through him now, and he understood the guilt his father always felt about Edith. Just like Mac hadn't been there for her when she'd needed him, Thorne felt like he hadn't, either.

"Why didn't you tell me that you're going to be working here?" he asked.

"I wasn't at liberty to say," she replied.

"At liberty?" He snorted, and his guilt turned to frustration. He remembered why nobody helped Edith—because just as her mother had with Mac, she never asked for it, never admitted she needed it. "You work for a real estate development firm, not the CIA. Why the hell aren't you at liberty to say?"

She glared at him. "I have a confidentiality agreement with my employer."

"That agreement says you can't even tell anyone who you work for?"

She nodded.

And he cursed. "Maybe you do work for the CIA, although I can't imagine what the hell they'd want with this place." He turned toward the house and shook his head. "I can't imagine what anyone wants with this place."

She said nothing but he wasn't certain if that was because she wasn't at liberty to say, or if it was because she didn't know.

"There's a hell of a lot of work to do here," he continued. "You can't handle all of this alone." Was her employer going to send reinforcements or expect her to do everything herself?

She sighed and nodded. "That's true. I can't."

He widened his eyes in astonishment. "I can't believe you're actually admitting you can't do everything alone."

She lifted her chin and bristled with pride. "I can do everything…but plumbing and fixing the AC. I need to hire someone to do that."

"Rafferty Construction—"

"River offered to work here," Edith said.

"River?" He glanced at the house again, surprised that his brother would consider working here. That he would even want to be around this place and its memories ever again. "He's been working at the ranch."

"He said you don't really need him."

"That's not it." Thorne sighed. "We've been taking it easy on him. We don't know how badly he's injured."

She nodded. "He was right."

"About what?"

"The pity," she replied. "He thinks everybody pities him."

They had several reasons for feeling that way. He'd been hurt in the line of duty, and he'd been hurt again when he'd returned home to find out the man he'd believed was his dad wasn't. A DNA test had confirmed Wes Kingston's suspicion that he wasn't River's father. But nobody knew who was. Maybe not even Livia herself. Poor River...

"Do you pity him?" Thorne asked. "Is that why you'd hire him?"

"I would hire him because I don't think he's going to bother me to find out who my boss is," she said. "I don't think he's going to talk to the press, either."

Thorne chuckled. "That's the last thing he'd do." He didn't want any media attention. That was why they'd all promised to keep it secret that he didn't know who his father was.

"Can I trust him?" Edith asked.

"I just said he won't go to the press—"

"I'm not talking about that," Edith said. "I just want to know that he's a man I can trust. We'll be working alone together in this house."

"Of course," Thorne said. "River's a man of honor. A hero."

"Thanks for being my hero right now," Edith told him with a hug. But she pulled away from him and headed back toward the house.

Knowing he was being dismissed, Thorne headed toward his truck. As he drove away, he wondered about what he'd told her. He wondered if River could be trusted. His brother had been gone ten years. How well did any of them really know him?

After whatever he'd been through, how well did River even know himself?

Chapter 6

Her hands trembled as she reached for the stallion's reins. River wasn't sure which one of them was more skittish, the woman or the horse. Jade expelled a shaky breath and smoothed her hand over the mane. It wasn't Shadow making his younger sister nervous.

Jade was an expert horsewoman. Hell, she'd been born riding. And she'd trained horses far more temperamental than Shadow.

"What's wrong?" he asked her as she began to lead the stallion around the pasture outside Mac's barn. He'd offered to bring the horse to her, but she'd wanted to work with it here. Trailering him was too traumatic, probably bringing up all those times he had been trailered from racetrack to racetrack.

River was able to relate to the traumatic memories. At least his only came back in dreams—when his guard was down and he couldn't fight them. Edith had helped him fight that morning, when she'd held him. He couldn't forget the feeling of her bare arms wrapped around him.

But when she'd needed him, after all those reporters had stormed the property, he hadn't been there for her. He shuddered at the memory of the camera bulbs flashing through the ivy-covered window, of the voices raised with questions. He would rather have faced a firing squad than that. But he hadn't left until Thorne had shown up to help her.

And she'd had her can of pepper spray for protection. Edith Beaulieu was tougher than her slim build and beauty suggested.

"Where are you?" Jade called out to him, concern in her soft voice and eyes.

"What?" he asked as he blinked his one good eye to focus on his sister's tense face. She looked thinner since he'd first returned and more haunted than he did.

"You looked like you were a million miles away," she said. And she was obviously thinking he'd been back *there*—to the scene of that last explosion.

He shook his head. "Not nearly that far," he assured her. "Just next door."

She tensed even more and all the color drained from her face. It was acres away but she glanced in the direction of the estate and asked, "To La Bonne Vie?"

He nodded now.

She shuddered. "What the hell were you doing there?"

"That's what I'd like to know," a husky female voice remarked with that sexy Louisiana drawl that had River's stomach muscles and other parts of his body tensing.

He turned toward Edith where she stood on the other

side of the corral fence. "I told you—I was making sure the place was safe."

"There's nothing safe about that place," Jade remarked, and as her nerves increased, the horse reared up. "Shh…" she told him. But her usual skills had no effect on the scared animal.

Dodging the raised hooves, River ducked in and grabbed the reins from his sister. Using all his strength, he tugged the horse down and led it back into the barn. When he returned after putting the stallion into his stall, he found Jade and Edith deep in conversation.

His sister seemed even more agitated. "What have you said to her?" River asked Edith, as he hurried to Jade's side and wrapped his arm around her trembling shoulders. Since Jade had never left Shadow Creek, she had probably met Edith several times before Thorne's wedding, so the women knew each other. Did they not like each other?

"It's what she hasn't said," Jade replied. "She won't answer me about what the new owner's plans are for La Bonne Vie."

"She can't," River said.

Jade snorted, much like one of her horses might. "Yeah, right…"

"It's true," he insisted.

And Edith turned toward him, her brown eyes wide with obvious surprise over his defense of her.

"She has a confidentiality agreement," he explained. "She could risk losing her job."

"She's risking a hell of a lot more by spending time in that house," Jade ominously warned him.

"What do you mean?" Edith asked her.

Jade trembled. "Nothing good ever happened in that house."

River could remember some good times—with his siblings, with Mac, with some of the nannies and tutors Livia had hired for them. He could even remember a few good times with their mother—when she'd paid them attention.

"Come on, Jade," he admonished his sister. "You know that's not completely true—"

"Maybe not for you," she said. "But it's true for me. I hate that house. I hope the new owner burns down the entire place!"

"Jade!" River exclaimed, shocked at his sister's outburst.

She tugged free of his arm around her shoulders and stepped out the gate. A pang struck his heart as he was torn between chasing after his sister and staying to talk to Edith.

River had been gone so long that he barely knew Jade. She'd been a child when he'd joined the Marines. But if Jade was anything like him, she would prefer to be alone to get herself back under control. At least River had always preferred to be alone—until that morning, when he'd surfaced from the nightmare to find Edith holding him.

He stared after Jade as she headed toward her truck. He wasn't sure what he would say to her if he followed her. He didn't understand why she hated La Bonne Vie so much. Sure, he wasn't a huge fan himself, but it was just a house, after all. He turned his attention to Edith, who stood on the other side of the fence and asked, "Should I go after her?"

She was staring after his sister, too, her usually smooth brow furrowed. "She does seem awfully upset."

Instead of squeezing between the fence, River put one hand on top and vaulted over it. Then he headed toward the truck as Jade was backing up. She slammed on the brakes and rolled down the window as he approached.

"Hey," he said. "What's going on with you?"

She shook her head, sending her ponytail swinging from side to side. "Nothing."

"If you ever want to talk…" Even as he uttered the words, he realized he was being a hypocrite and grimaced.

"Do you?" she challenged him. "I'll talk when you do."

Before he could say anything, she rolled up the window and drove away, gravel spewing beneath the truck tires. Maybe she was just in a hurry to get back to her ranch. She rarely left it.

"Guess she didn't want to talk," Edith mused as she walked away from the fence and joined him in the middle of the driveway.

He shook his head.

"I'm sorry," she said.

"Why?" He was the one who owed her the apology for leaving her alone with the ruthless reporters.

"I didn't realize that my working up at the house might cause issues with your family."

"It's not you," he said. "It's your boss. Not knowing who he is or what he wants with the place is what's making everyone uneasy."

"I thought that was Livia being on the loose," she

murmured. Then her eyes widened and she apologized again. "I shouldn't have said that."

He shrugged. "It's true. Not knowing where she is has everyone on edge, too."

"I thought she'd been sighted in Florida."

"That's what the media claims," he agreed.

"You don't believe them?"

He sighed. "I don't know what to believe when it comes to my mother." Like who the hell his father was. She'd lied to him about that his entire life.

She uttered a heavy sigh of her own, as if she understood. "Since it bothers your sister so much, are you sure you want a job working at La Bonne Vie?"

"Are you offering me one?" he asked.

She sighed again—in resignation. "You have one— if you want it."

His heart rate quickened with anticipation, and not just over being able to search the house. He was probably more excited about the prospect of working with Edith Beaulieu.

A bulb flashed as the camera took another photo. No reporter was taking these pictures, though. Edith controlled the camera, taking photos of each item she uncovered in the house. Some had been damaged; pictures torn from frames, vases shattered. The FBI's search had been excessively thorough. Excessive because Edith wasn't certain what—if anything—of the personal property was salvageable.

"Why did you buy this?" she murmured. But Declan was nowhere around to answer her question, and she breathed a sigh of relief that she would have some time before his visit to get the house ready for him.

But would she have enough time—if she didn't have help? She'd offered River the job yesterday, but he hadn't officially accepted. He'd only nodded at her. Maybe that was the cowboy agreement? She would have preferred a handshake. But then, touching him wasn't the best idea. She'd only touched him that once—in his bedroom above the stables—and she couldn't forget the feeling of his skin beneath her fingertips, the rippling of his muscles beneath the flesh glistening with perspiration.

She shuddered as she remembered how he'd looked—how incredibly muscular he was. Male perfection. The scar, the patch…they only added to the sexiness that was River Colton.

She lifted a book from the floor and used it to fan herself. The first thing she needed to have done was get the air conditioner repaired—if it was repairable.

The front door rattled as someone turned the knob. Actually, the first thing she needed to have fixed was the gate; it needed to be secured so no more reporters could trespass on the property. She drew her pepper spray from her purse. This time she wouldn't hesitate to use it. Maybe if the word got out that she was armed, the media would stop harassing her.

She could only hope…

She stood at the bottom of the curved stairwell, facing the foyer and the extra-tall exterior door. It slowly opened, pouring sunshine across the marble floor. But then a long shadow swallowed the sun. It could have been Mac or Thorne or River. But she figured they would have knocked first or rung the bell to let her know they'd arrived.

"What do you think you're doing!" she demanded as she rushed forward with the canister of pepper spray.

"Working," a deep voice drawled. "Isn't that what you expect your employees to do?"

As he stepped farther into the foyer, and the sunshine washed away the shadows, it was clear he'd been working. He'd taken off his shirt. The sweat-damp garment hung over one broad shoulder. His chest was bare, but for the dog tags, and slick with sweat.

"You—you've been working," she stammered as her mouth began to water. She'd thought it was hot before. But his stepping inside had raised the temperature even more.

He stepped closer, close enough that she could smell him—the sweat, the musk, the man…

He reached out, and her heart slammed against her ribs. But instead of touching her, he held something out to her.

"What is this?" she asked as she dropped her pepper spray into her purse and accepted the black plastic thing he handed her. She stared down at the thing he'd dropped into her palm as if he'd been afraid to touch her. It looked like a garage door opener.

"It's for the gate," he said. "I fixed it, so you won't have to worry about trespassers anymore."

She suspected he'd been more worried than she'd been—about the reporters. She still had an odd feeling that she wasn't alone in the house—even before he'd joined her. She couldn't quite shake that strange sensation she'd had ever since she'd first noticed that gleaming in the dark the first night she'd come to the house.

What had been at the bottom of the stairs? Just an animal?

She'd stumbled across a few inside the house—living and dead. She wasn't sure which she dreaded finding more. She shuddered and murmured, "Now if you could find a way to keep out the other animals."

He nodded. "I noticed a couple broken windows. I'm sure that's how they're getting inside. I'll fix those next unless—" he stopped and stared down at her "—there's something else you'd rather have me do…"

Me. The naughty thought flitted through her mind, shocking her. She was usually all business—nothing but professional. And she especially needed to maintain that professionalism with River Colton. She had never mixed business with pleasure before, and she certainly didn't intend to start now.

She couldn't deny, though, that it would be pleasurable to be with him, to be able to kiss him and touch him and have him kiss and touch her. She shivered despite the heat. Then she expelled a ragged breath and pushed away the tempting thoughts of making love with River Colton.

It would never happen.

They both had too much work to do. On the house.

And she suspected that River had other work to do—on himself, so he could recover from his physical and emotional injuries. She couldn't help him with any of that; she hadn't been able to help her mother. Even professionals weren't able to help her mother. She couldn't go through that again. So she shook her head.

River lifted his shirt from his shoulder and swabbed at his face and chest. "Maybe I should take a look at the air conditioner first," he suggested.

"Um, um…" She wasn't in such a hurry to get it fixed now—not if it meant that he'd be putting on his shirt again. She had no intention of giving in to her desire to kiss and touch him. But she could still look.

She could still admire his masculine perfection.

"Okay, windows first," he said. "I'll make sure nothing else gets inside the house." He headed toward the door.

But even after he'd stepped outside and closed the door behind himself, Edith didn't feel alone. "What about what's already inside?" she asked.

Would he take care of those intruders, too? But what if those intruders weren't the rodents she hoped they were? She remembered his sister's dire warning—that Edith spending time in this house put her at risk. Of what?

Losing her life?

River walked past one of the windows, and the sunlight glistened off the sweat streaking down his muscular chest and broad back.

Or losing her heart?

Pride swelled in Knox's heart as he watched his son spur the horse on to gallop around the riding ring. He leaned over the railing, his shoulder nearly touching his sister's as she leaned next to him.

"He's a natural," Jade said. Her pride in her nephew was obvious.

She had reason for pride. She'd taught the boy how to ride—even before she'd known for sure that Cody was a Colton.

A twinge of regret struck Knox now—for all the years of his son's life that he'd missed. But he shook off the regret. He couldn't change the past, but he could make sure that he was present every day for his son now.

"He's had a good teacher," Knox praised his sister. "Thank you for being part of his life."

Jade reached out and squeezed his arm. "It's not your fault," she said.

"I know."

"It's Livia's," Jade said, and there was resentment and something else in her voice. Fear.

His mother had manipulated him and Allison when they were young. But he couldn't lay all the blame on her. He couldn't blame Allison, either. She'd only been trying to protect their son from being a Colton and all the drama that caused. It was his job to protect him now.

"How is the investigation going?" she asked.

He shrugged and reminded her, "I'm not a Ranger anymore."

"You should be."

"No."

"But you are a lawman," she said.

He agreed. But he didn't want to go back to the Rangers—not now that he had a family. He didn't want to miss another minute of his son's life. "I'll figure something out."

He had an idea. But he needed to talk to his wife about it first. They had promised to keep nothing from each other ever again.

"Will River?" Jade asked.

"Will River what?"

"Figure something out," she said. "He seems lost."

Knox sighed. He'd noticed that, too. But he didn't know how to help him. Cody wasn't the only one of whose life Knox had missed ten years. His youngest brother had been gone that long, and even though he'd returned, there was something missing. He seemed like a stranger to them all.

Jade lowered her voice to a conspiratorial whisper and murmured, "He's been going over to La Bonne Vie."

Knox tensed. "The property's been sold. He's trespassing."

"I don't think Edith Beaulieu is going to press charges."

Knox had seen *Everything's Blogger*'s latest post complete with a photo of Edith outside La Bonne Vie. "What's Mac's niece got to do with the estate?" he asked.

"She works for the new owner."

"Who is it?"

"She won't say," Jade replied, and the resentment was back. "She won't say who it is or what he or she wants with the estate."

Knox shrugged. "Who cares?"

Jade gasped. "I care."

"Why?" Was she trying to hang on to fond memories of the house or dispel bad ones?

"And I don't want River spending time in that house," she said with a grimace and wrinkled her nose.

"Nothing's going to happen to him there," Knox assured her. "River's home. He's safe."

Jade shook her head, which had her ponytail swinging across her shoulders. "Nobody's safe at La Bonne Vie."

He didn't have great memories of growing up there, but he didn't have horrible ones, either. Of course his father hadn't died there—like Jade's had. A horse had killed Fabrizio, though, not the house. Concern for his son had him turning his attention back to the ring. But Cody rode with ease and confidence.

How could Jade work with horses after what had happened to her father? But maybe that was why she did, so she could make sure nothing like that would happen to anyone else.

He wound his arm around her thin shoulders and offered a reassuring squeeze. "River will be fine."

Jade just shook her head. "Nobody is safe anywhere—until Livia is back behind bars."

That much was probably true. Their mother was a dangerous, unpredictable woman. While there had been sightings of her in Florida, nobody knew for certain that was where she was. Hell, she could be anywhere.

Chapter 7

River flinched as he shoved his arms into the sleeves of the cotton shirt. His shoulders and back ached from all the work he'd been doing at La Bonne Vie. But those weren't the only parts of his body that ached. There was tension gathered lower that intensified every time he saw or even thought of Edith Beaulieu.

Heat flashed through his body, chasing away the last of the chill from his cold shower. He glanced toward the open bathroom door and thought about taking another. Then he heard the footsteps on the stairs, leading up from the barn. Someone was coming.

Usually he dreaded visitors, as uncomfortable as they were with how they couldn't look directly at him as if they didn't know whether to meet his one good eye or stare at the patch. But now his pulse quickened with anticipation. Was it Edith? Had she thought of something to tell him about the house? Another chore for him to perform?

She'd sounded like she'd meant it earlier—when she'd sent him home with orders to take the night off. She'd said he'd been working too hard.

What about her?

In the week he'd been working with her at La Bonne Vie, he'd rarely seen her take a break. She toiled tirelessly, inventorying every damn item she found in the estate—examining every room.

But for the secret ones. She hadn't found those. And neither had River. Because of Edith, he hadn't had a chance to look. She was always there. Except maybe now.

Maybe now she was here.

He needed to be *there*, then. He needed to get back inside the house to continue his search. He was pretty sure he'd found a secret room off the wine cellar. He needed to get inside it—to see if Livia had stashed anything there. Anything that might help him find out who the hell he was.

But if Edith was *here*, he didn't want to be there. He wanted to be wherever she was. He reached for the buttons on his shirt just as the door creaked open. He was surprised that she'd walk in without knocking. But she had that day she'd held him through the end of his nightmare. Or maybe she'd knocked and he just hadn't heard it.

He glanced up and disappointment flashed through him. "Hey, Thorne…"

His brother stepped inside, closed the door and leaned against it. Then he crossed his arms over his chest and glared at River.

"What?" he asked. It was clear his brother was angry with him. "What the hell did I do?"

"It's what you haven't done," Thorne replied.

River groaned as realization and guilt dawned on him. "I'm sorry. I know I should be helping you and Mac out around here—since you're letting me stay here and—"

Thorne held up a hand. "This is your home," he said. "You don't have to work to stay here."

"Then what are you mad about?" River asked. "What haven't I done?"

"You haven't stopped Edith from working herself into the ground," Thorne said. "You're supposed to be helping her over there. I vouched for you—"

"You vouched for me?" he interrupted.

"I told Edith she could trust you."

He nearly flinched. But he hadn't asked his brother to lie for him. Of course Thorne had had no idea he was lying. He didn't know River's real reason for wanting to work at La Bonne Vie. And if he learned the truth, he would probably be furious that River hadn't been open and honest about his intentions. Of course, if Thorne had known the truth, he probably wouldn't have vouched for him.

"Thank you," he murmured.

"Don't thank me," Thorne said. "I think I made a horrible mistake."

Had his brother figured out that River had ulterior motives? But now those motives didn't include just being around La Bonne Vie. He wanted to be around Edith, too—to breathe in that unique fragrance that was hers alone, to watch her as she moved with an innate grace around the house.

"Has Edith complained about me?" River asked as dread clutched his stomach muscles into knots.

Maybe he'd unnerved her with his presence. Maybe she couldn't stand looking at him and his scars.

But she looked at him often. He caught her studying him as much as he probably studied her. Her interest helped his healing in a way that medical attention and time had not. The way she looked at him almost made him feel whole again.

But that was ridiculous…

"No," Thorne replied. "I'm complaining."

"Yeah, I get that," River said. "But I don't know what you're complaining about. I've been helping her as much as I can over there."

"Too much," Thorne said. "You've got the house ready enough for her to move in."

"What?" He'd done a lot of work in the past week, but there was still a lot left to do.

Thorne unfolded his arms from across his chest, and the glare left his face. "You didn't know?"

"She didn't say anything about it," River said. But she'd obviously told him to leave early in order to get him out of her way. "She told you?"

Thorne shook his head. "I just happened to stop by the B and B in town as she was checking out of her room."

River groaned. Now how the hell was he going to search for those secret rooms?

"I see you're no happier about the idea than I am," Thorne remarked. He narrowed his eyes and studied River. "Why aren't you?"

"I don't think it's safe for her to be there alone," he admitted.

"You really think she saw something that first night?" Thorne asked.

River nodded.

"What was it?"

He shrugged. "I don't know."

"You didn't see anything yourself?"

"Not really," he admitted. He'd seen a glimmer of something, but with his vision being compromised, he wasn't certain it had really been there. "But the way she screamed…she must have seen something."

Thorne's brow was furrowed with the same skepticism with which he'd studied River's face.

"You don't think she saw anything?" he asked.

Instead of answering his question, Thorne asked one of his own. "Has Edith told you about her mom?"

"No." They'd talked about the house, about the damage the FBI search had done. They didn't talk about personal things—as if they were both trying really hard to keep their relationship professional.

"My aunt has some issues," Thorne said. "Some serious ones."

River snorted. "Don't we all…?"

"Not like these," Thorne said. "She's been institutionalized for most of Edith's life."

"Oh…" The dread moved from his stomach to his heart, clutching it.

"So you see why I'm concerned," Thorne continued.

River shook his head. "Actually I don't."

"If Edith is seeing things…"

Anger surged through him. "Edith isn't seeing things," he hotly defended her. "And you, of all people, should know better than to judge someone by what her mother has done."

Thorne flinched. "You're right. You're right. None of us are killers just because our mother is."

Speak for yourself... The words burned the back of River's throat, but he kept them to himself. He didn't want to think about what he'd had to do—let alone talk about it.

"It's just that Aunt Merrilee sees things, too, that aren't there," Thorne continued. "She started exhibiting the symptoms after Edith's dad died and got diagnosed when she was committed."

River couldn't imagine how hard that must have been on her daughter. He wanted to ask questions, wanted to know what had happened to Edith. But Thorne was already talking again.

"When Mac found out, he figured she might have been misdiagnosed," Thorne continued. "But by the time Mac did find out, she'd been moved to a better psychiatric facility and the diagnosis was confirmed. She has schizophrenia. That's a disease that's oftentimes hereditary."

"But you and Mac don't have it," River said.

Thorne shook his head. "No."

"Edith doesn't have it, either," River assured his brother. "She saw something that night."

Thorne released a ragged breath of relief. "Yeah, yeah, you're right. It was probably an animal, huh?"

River nodded. "I've found quite a few of them in the house." A possum, a raccoon, a squirrel and of course the mice. But he wasn't certain it was an animal Edith had seen.

Or if there was something else in that house—or someone else...

The woman was already back. Why did she never leave for long?

She must not have seen anything that first night

she'd showed up at La Bonne Vie—or she would have called the police. And she wouldn't keep coming back.

Tonight she had returned with a suitcase. She intended to move in.

That would not do.

Her presence would make things more difficult, make it harder to remain undetected. But getting rid of her would draw attention to the estate, too. The police would come then—to investigate the young woman's murder.

The knife dropped back onto the bureau—next to the gun. No. Neither weapon could be used.

The only way to get rid of Edith Beaulieu without drawing attention would be an *accident*. The house was in disrepair. The young woman was alone in it.

Accidents were bound to happen.

Sooner rather than later.

Thorne thought she was seeing things. Edith hadn't missed the speculation in his eyes as he'd studied her like a psychiatrist studied a patient, trying to determine how great a danger she posed to herself or others. Edith knew that look well; she'd watched her mother be evaluated so many times.

And every time Merrilee had been deemed a danger to herself. She would never harm anyone else—not like Thorne's mother had hurt people. So many people had been hurt because of that woman. Edith should have pointed out to her cousin that she wasn't about to judge him because of what his mother was. So he had no right to judge her.

But she understood his concern. She was concerned herself.

She dropped her suitcase onto the bed in the master suite River had repaired. The bathroom functioned, like the powder room on the main floor. Leaving her suitcase unpacked, she hurried down the back stairs to the kitchen, where she'd left a bag of groceries on the counter. River had also gotten that room operational again, too. He impressed her with everything he'd accomplished in a week.

But she had not done nearly as much as she'd wanted, as she'd intended. She'd let him distract her from her responsibilities. That was why she'd had to move in—because it would take working around the clock to get the inventory done in time for Declan's visit.

She couldn't let River distract her anymore. Maybe she would have to let him go. He'd done what she'd wanted—gotten the place inhabitable. But the thought of firing him had her stomach churning with dread.

Or was it fear?

She still didn't like being alone in the house—except that she never felt truly alone. Even now…

River was gone. He'd assured her he'd gotten rid of all the creatures inside, as well. So what was that creaking noise she heard?

He'd cut back the vines over the windows and the branches from the roof. So what could it be?

Had he missed something? Or someone?

She'd left her purse on the counter next to that bag of groceries, so she pulled out the canister of pepper spray and her cell phone. Of course the noise came from the basement. She could have called for help—could have called River or her uncle Mac or even Thorne. But

River had already investigated the basement several times, and he had never found anything.

She hadn't found anyone but him. So she wasn't too concerned about investigating again. She slid her phone into the pocket of her jeans, so she could hold on to the pepper spray as she opened the basement door. Her hand trembled as she turned the knob and opened the door. She flipped on the light switch and chased away the shadows.

The dampness remained, making her shiver as she descended the steps. She was grateful now that she'd put on jeans when she'd changed back at the B and B. She probably should have worn more than a T-shirt with them, but it was still warm outside. Fortunately, River had fixed the air conditioner.

Apparently there was nothing the man could not do. He was extremely smart and good with his hands. She thought of those hands—those big, strong hands touching her like he touched his tools. And she shivered again.

Then something clanged, distracting her, and the sound echoed throughout the cavernous space. It sounded like that noise she'd heard the day she'd found River with the crowbar in his hand.

What had he been up to that day?

And had he returned despite her telling him to knock off for the day?

"Hello?" she called out. Her voice trembled like her hands. "River?"

If she caught him again, she would have no qualms about firing him. She couldn't work with someone she couldn't trust.

She couldn't lust after him, either. And she'd been

doing entirely too much of that. She expelled a ragged sigh of resignation. She would have to fire him— whether or not she found him down there.

Another clang rang out.

"River?" she called out. She hoped he was the one making the noise.

Because if it wasn't him...

Who the hell was it?

His fixing the gate had stopped any more reporters from trespassing. He'd repaired all the broken windows, too, so no more animals should have been able to get inside...unless he hadn't found all the ones who'd already taken up residence in the abandoned house.

She shuddered at the thought of coming upon more rodents or wildlife. She'd found enough living and dead carcasses to last her a lifetime.

Maybe it was time she asked Declan for a raise. Or combat pay. Yeah, she needed a raise. She thought about taking her phone out of her pocket to call Declan. Or someone else—someone who could help her. But what would she tell them? That she heard some clanging noise, which was probably just old pipes rattling? She continued down the corridor leading away from the stairs. The light was dim, coming only from sconces on the stone walls.

She didn't hear any more clanging, but she continued to the room where she'd found River that day with the crowbar. It was a wine cellar—full yet of racks and crates. But only a few dust-covered bottles remained. She had yet to inventory down here. But maybe she would find something of value, something vintage collectors sought.

She moved between the racks and lifted a bottle.

After slipping her pepper spray into her pocket, she brushed off the label. She was no expert on wine, but she did prefer reds. And this was a Beaujolais.

A smile played across her mouth. Would Declan miss this one bottle?

Or would he agree that she deserved it for all the hard work she'd already done? Her mouth began to water, like it had the day River had walked shirtless into the house.

Damn that man…

She couldn't get him off her mind even after sending him away. Would she be able to stop thinking about him if she fired him? Or would she continue fantasizing about him?

Hell, maybe Thorne had been right to worry about her. Maybe she was losing her mind. For the first time in her life she couldn't stop thinking about a man.

And she kept hearing things.

Then she heard it again, but it was a softer clang now. And she saw something, just a shadow moving across the stones behind the racks.

She fumbled for her pepper spray, but before she could pull it out, the racks tipped forward, tumbling onto each other like dominoes. Edith had no time to move—no time to escape—before they fell on her, knocking her to the concrete floor. Something struck her head, maybe a rack, maybe a bottle.

She didn't see it. She only heard the sharp crack and felt the flash of pain before everything—blessedly—went numb and dark.

Chapter 8

River squinted against the morning sun as he slid the key in the lock of the front door. Despite Edith sending him home early the day before, he should have come back last night—when Thorne had informed him she intended to stay at La Bonne Vie. It wasn't like he'd been able to relax like she'd told him to—not once he'd learned she was alone in the house.

But he knew how independent she was and that she would probably get angry if he acted as if she needed protecting.

After unlocking the door, he pushed it open and sunlight poured in. He glanced toward the curved stairwell, almost expecting to see his mother there. She used to love making an entrance, descending from the second floor on those steps. But she wasn't there. She was hiding out somewhere. Florida? He doubted it.

Maybe Paris or Rome or some private island…

He didn't care. He wasn't looking for her.

"Edith!" he called out. He'd showed up early, but he still expected her to be up and bustling about—taking pictures, cataloging personal property. "Edith?" He peered around the house but saw no movement beyond the dust particles dancing in the sunlight.

So he bounded up those stairs to the second floor. She'd had him get the master suite ready first. He'd thought she'd wanted it inhabitable for her boss. But when he headed down the hall and looked through the open double doors, it was her suitcase he saw on the bed. At least he assumed the purple paisley suitcase belonged to her.

He was pretty sure, from the conversation he'd overheard, that her boss was a man. But maybe that was sexist of him to think so and to assume the suitcase was hers.

It wasn't open but it didn't look as though it had been unpacked. The closet doors stood open, the hangers empty. The bed hadn't been slept in, either. In fact, the sheets she must have brought for the new mattress were still in the packages next to the suitcase.

His heart began to pound faster as a frisson of concern chased down his spine. "Edith?" he called out again.

Her car was in the driveway. And Thorne had seen her checking out of the B and B in town well before bedtime. She would've had to sleep here, and this was the only room that was ready for occupation.

"Edith?"

He hurried down the back stairwell that came out in the kitchen. Like the bedroom, it was empty, too.

But a bag of groceries sat on the counter, the bottom of the cloth bag damp with whatever had melted inside it. She hadn't even put them away. Her purse sat next to the bag.

"Edith?" he shouted. Then he noticed the basement door standing open, and his heart slammed against his ribs. Of course she would have gone down there again.

What the hell had she heard or seen now?

He hesitated before stepping forward or looking down. What if he found her there, sprawled at the bottom of the steps? Bracing himself, he peered down, but there was no body lying on the concrete floor— nothing but his own shadow.

"Edith?" he yelled as he rushed down the stairs. He glanced into the mechanical room. Maybe she'd had to check the breakers again or something. But the room was empty. So he turned the other way and headed down the hallway.

The farther he went with no sign of her, the more anxious he felt. Where the hell had she gone?

Then he remembered where she'd found him that day he'd been certain he'd discovered another secret room. The wine cellar. He hurried past the stone walls to the arch that opened into that corner of the basement. And his breath left his lungs as shock overwhelmed him. The racks had fallen over—along with a pile of crates.

What the hell had happened down there?

The crowbar he'd been using that day lay beside the first overturned rack. But it was near the wall he'd been prying at, so maybe that was where he'd left it.

"Edith?"

The pile of debris shifted, and a wine bottle rolled

out from beneath the overturned racks. As it rolled, it left a trail of red wine and a smear of something thicker, maybe blood, across the concrete.

His heart slammed against his ribs as realization dawned on him. Edith was beneath that pile. Heedless of their weight, he pulled the racks aside, tossing them against the stone walls as he sought to uncover her. She lay sprawled across the concrete, her arm raised over her face as if to protect herself. But a small pool of blood had formed beneath her head, sticking her thick black hair to the cement.

He dropped to his knees beside her. His hand trembled as he reached out and felt her throat, looking for a pulse. Her smooth skin was cold—so cold—but her pulse fluttered beneath his fingertips. Then her lashes fluttered as her eyes opened. She stared up at him, her brow furrowing with confusion. As the skin pulled at the wound on her forehead, she flinched.

"Are you all right?" he asked, his voice thick and gruff as concern overwhelmed him.

She reached up and touched the wound. It had stopped bleeding, but it looked swollen. And she must have been unconscious a long time. Or maybe she just hadn't been strong enough to get the racks off her.

"Does anything else hurt?" he asked. He skimmed his hands over her arms and legs, looking for broken bones.

She sucked in a breath. But he couldn't tell if she was in pain or shock. Probably both...

"I need to call 9-1-1," he said. But as he reached for his cell phone, she grabbed his wrist.

"No," she murmured. "I don't need an ambulance." As if to prove her point, she struggled to sit up.

River grasped her shoulders to steady her. "Take it easy. You could have some broken bones. That's why you need to get to the ER." He knew what it was like to have injuries you weren't even aware of. He'd had no idea he'd lost his eye…until he'd seen the horror on the faces of the medics who'd rushed to his aid.

"I don't need to go," she insisted, and she sounded a little stronger now. She even seemed steadier as she braced herself on his shoulders and stood up. But then she swayed and fell against his chest.

He swung her up in his arms. She didn't protest now. She just laid her head on his shoulder and he felt the stickiness of her blood-soaked hair against his neck.

Emotion constricted his lungs, making it hard for him to draw a deep breath. What if she'd had no pulse? What if he'd found her too late to help her? Like he had been too late to help Henry…

Images flashed through his mind of that horrific day, of the horrific things that had happened. And sweat beaded on his lip and his brow as his body began to tremble. But he forced himself to breathe, to focus on the present and forget the past. The might-have-beens…

He couldn't think about the horror. He had to focus instead on getting her help and then on making sure she stayed safe. As he carried her from the wine cellar, he glanced back through the arched doorway at the racks and crates strewn across the floor where she'd lain. A few wine bottles and her canister of pepper spray littered the floor, along with something else— something that looked like her cell phone. She must have dropped it when the racks knocked her down. How had they fallen?

What the hell had happened?

* * *

Warmth spread through Edith. Maybe it was the IV the nurse had given her to replenish whatever fluids she might have lost after spending the night on the floor of the wine cellar. Or maybe it was embarrassment over River carrying her into Shadow Creek Memorial Hospital.

If it was the IV, she welcomed it. Her skin was so chilled she thought she'd never get warm again. But if it was embarrassment…

She had every reason for it. She hated how weak and helpless she must have looked when River carried her into the ER. He had drawn the attention of not only the hospital staff but also of everyone else in the place. Unfortunately, that had included a reporter who'd used his phone to snap pictures of them, until a security guard had escorted him out.

But his phone hadn't been taken, so those photos were bound to be posted somewhere. She needed to call Declan—to warn him—but she didn't have her phone, either. It must have fallen out of her pocket when the racks had knocked her down. But River had been so hell-bent on getting her medical attention that he would have refused to stop to look for it or anything else.

He must have run three red lights on his way to the hospital. And Shadow Creek probably only had those three traffic signals. But for as anxious as he'd been to get her there, he hadn't been anxious to stay. As soon as he'd laid her on the gurney a nurse had brought, he'd stepped back.

She'd thought he'd only done that so the doctor could treat her. But when the medical staff had moved away to order tests and retrieve IVs, she hadn't seen him.

He'd disappeared. Maybe he'd only gone to the waiting room, though.

Or had that reporter scared him off? He was even more averse to the media than Declan was and that was saying something. She could understand River's reasons, given his injuries and his family history.

But what was Declan's reason for hating media attention? She'd known him a long time—ever since Child Protective Services had brought her to the foster home where he'd been living. He was like a brother to her, but an older brother who didn't share as much with her as she shared with him. Like he'd said, it was hard for him to trust, and he probably trusted her more than anyone else.

But she didn't even know what he wanted with La Bonne Vie—despite risking her life for the damn place. What the hell had happened the night before?

Everything was hazy now. She'd gone down to check out a noise. But she hadn't seen anything. Or had she? Had there been a shadow against the stone wall just before the racks had fallen?

Of course that could have been her own damn shadow. The light was dim down in the cellar, making it hard to see anything clearly. And now her head pounded as she tried to remember…

She closed her eyes to focus on the elusive memory.

"Oh, my God," a deep voice exclaimed. "Are you all right?"

She opened her eyes to see her uncle leaning over the gurney, his face taut with concern. And she knew where River had gone—to call Mac. All the Colton kids were used to going to Mac for help. She felt a flash of resentment that they had been able to while he was her uncle and she couldn't call him.

But that was because her mother had made her promise. The visions, the voices—that had been their secret. And Edith's nightmare. She shivered.

"River said he found you on the basement floor," Mac said. "Did you spend the entire night down there?"

She must have—because the sun had been shining when River had carried her out to his truck. Morning had arrived. And when she'd gone downstairs, it had been night. "Yes."

He dragged the blanket up over her shoulders. "You must be completely chilled from lying on that cold concrete floor." He reached out toward the wound on her forehead but drew his fingers back before he touched it. "And you were hurt. Did you lose consciousness?"

"I don't remember..." And the doctor hadn't told her anything yet, not until she had more tests.

"Then you must have," Uncle Mac said. "You shouldn't have been at the house by yourself. It's too dangerous."

She couldn't argue that now. She couldn't argue at all with how violently her head pounded. "I don't know exactly what happened..."

But the pounding in her head reminded her of the clanging noise that had drawn her downstairs. It had sounded like it had the day she'd found River in the wine cellar. Could he have been down there last night? But his concern when he'd found her had seemed so genuine, like he really cared about her. So how could he have hurt her? But if he cared, where was he now?

"I don't know..."

An orderly stepped up behind Uncle Mac. "I need to bring you to Radiology now."

"For a CT scan?" Mac asked.

That was one of the tests the doctor had rattled off when he'd examined her. "It's not necessary," Edith said. "I'm fine now." Except for a persistent throbbing headache.

Mac squeezed her hand. "Let them thoroughly check you out," he urged her. "And make sure that you're really going to be okay."

She was fine but she wasn't certain she was going to be okay—not if that reporter posted the photo of River carrying her anywhere that Declan would see it. She could have asked to use her uncle's phone to call and warn her boss. But she knew that Declan wouldn't answer unless he recognized the number. And he wouldn't recognize Mac's.

She uttered a sigh of resignation. "Okay."

"Are you afraid of confined spaces?" the orderly asked as he wheeled her away.

"No…" But she trailed off as she realized that was a lie now. A memory flashed through her mind, of lying beneath that pile of racks and crates—being confined, being trapped. Helpless.

She shuddered. She had bigger fears now than of what Declan might think if he saw those photos. She had fears of being trapped…in La Bonne Vie.

Declan Sinclair hated *Everything's Blogger in Texas*. They were probably the slimiest of the internet tabloids. But while they might not get many other stories right, when it came to the Coltons they were surprisingly accurate and informed. So he clicked through to their site as he did at least once a day. And he gasped as he saw the photo dominating their front page.

"Edith!"

What the hell had happened to her? Blood matted the hair to one side of her forehead where she had a cut and a bruise. As if that wasn't bad enough, she was being carried—by River Colton.

The ex-Marine was easily recognizable, with the scars on the side of his face where the black patch covered his eye.

The headline read "Hero" Marine Carries Mysterious Woman into Shadow Creek Memorial's ER.

Edith wasn't the mystery. River Colton carrying her was. And the reporter must have had Declan's same doubts about how heroic the ex-Marine was, or he wouldn't have used the quotation marks. Had River hurt her?

Declan grabbed his phone from his desk and tapped on the contact for Edith. His call went directly to her voice mail. Was she still at the hospital?

He tried the number for Shadow Creek Memorial next, but they refused to release any information on patients to non–family members. Edith was his family, though. The only family he had—thanks to a Colton. Had another Colton taken her away from him?

He looked at the photo again, studying Edith's face. She didn't look frightened. In fact, she clung to River, her arms wrapped around his neck while her head nearly rested against his shoulder.

A sick feeling overwhelmed Declan.

"No…"

He would have understood had it been Thorne to whom she was clinging. Thorne was her cousin. But this Colton? River was nothing to Edith—nothing but trouble.

Guilt rushed over Declan next. He shouldn't have sent Edith to La Bonne Vie. He should have known—even with Livia sightings in Florida—that it was still too dangerous. Too many other Coltons lived around La Bonne Vie. Too many other Coltons posed a threat.

And somehow he suspected that this Colton, with his scars and his eye patch, proved the greatest threat to Edith of any of them.

Chapter 9

"So what do you think?" River asked as he watched his brother Knox move around the wine cellar. The former Texas Ranger leaned over the crowbar before returning to examine the racks and crates. "Did someone purposely knock these over onto Edith?"

And who the hell had done it? Because once River found out, he would take the person apart. Remembering how he'd found Edith, lying unconscious on the concrete, blood pooling beneath her head...

He shuddered with dread over what could have happened to her. But she was strong—so strong—that it would take more than a few racks and crates to take her out.

But why would anyone try?

"The crowbar certainly suggests it," Knox remarked. "Why else would it be here?"

Heat crawled up River's neck into his face. "Uh, I had the crowbar down here."

"Why?" Knox asked, glancing around the cellar before returning his attention to River. He studied him through narrowed eyes. "What were you doing with it?"

Trying to find the lever to open a door to a secret room. But he wasn't about to admit that to his big brother. Knox was so honorable that he would never approve of River's unauthorized searches of La Bonne Vie. But then, Knox had always known who he was.

And what he was. A lawman.

He was so good that River suddenly felt like a suspect. "Edith thought she saw something that first night she came to the house. And every once in a while…"

"What?" Knox asked.

"We hear stuff…" He gestured toward the crowbar. "That's why I had that—to check it out."

"Did you find anything?" Knox asked.

River shook his head. Not yet. Not what he was looking for. "The only intruders I've found are four-legged."

"And us," Knox said. "We don't have permission to actually be here, do we?"

"Hey, Ranger Colton, *I'm* not trespassing," River replied with a chuckle. "I work here, remember?"

"Why?" Knox asked.

He shrugged. "What else do I have to do?" He touched the patch. "Can't be a Marine anymore." At least he wouldn't be able to carry out the missions he once had. He probably would have been able to become an instructor or something. But he'd known it was time to come back to Shadow Creek and his family.

"There are a lot of other jobs out there that you could do," Knox said. "Allison would love to have you working for her."

He wanted to say that construction wasn't his calling. But that would raise even more questions about why he was working as a handyman.

A vibrating noise saved him from having to make any remark. He stepped closer to the overturned racks and spied the cell phone lying on the concrete. Leaning over, he picked it up. The contact on the screen just said Boss. He was tempted to tap the accept button and talk to the man, but before he could, the call disconnected.

That wasn't the only call Edith had missed from her boss. Several more came up on the screen.

"Can you find out who a number belongs to?" he asked Knox.

His brother shook his head. "Not anymore. I'm not a lawman."

"You should be," River said.

A slight smile curved Knox's mouth, and his blue eyes were even brighter than usual. "I've been thinking about it. But if I was again, I would have to have a reason to run that number. What would my reason be?"

"You don't want to know who bought La Bonne Vie?" River asked.

Knox shook his head. "I couldn't care less."

"Really?"

"Do you?" Knox asked. "Is that why you're working here? To find out who bought it and what they want to do with it?"

He didn't give a damn who the new owner was or what the hell he wanted to do with La Bonne Vie—as long as River found what he was looking for first. He glanced at the stone wall behind Knox.

He was sure there was a secret room behind that wall. He'd been so close...

That room was also close to where those racks had fallen over Edith. What if someone was inside?

A strange feeling rushed over River, raising the short hairs on the nape of his neck. He felt like someone else was there—listening to them.

"That's not why I'm working here," River insisted. "Like you, I couldn't care less what happens to this place."

"Then why are you working on it?" Knox asked the question but another, softer voice, echoed it.

"Why?" Edith asked.

River turned to where she stood under the arched doorway into the wine cellar. She must have been whom he'd sensed listening. He rushed over to her and put his hand on her shoulder to support her.

"You shouldn't be here," he said. "You should still be in the hospital."

She had a small bandage over the wound on her forehead. But her eyes looked clear and bright with curiosity and something else. Hurt?

Was she in physical or emotional pain?

He squeezed her shoulder, but she pulled back as if not wanting him to touch her. "What's wrong?" he asked with concern. "Are you all right?"

According to the ER doctor, Edith was fine. She'd suffered a slight concussion from whatever had hit her head, though. Fortunately, the painkillers had lessened the throbbing. It didn't pound as hard as her pulse, which had sped up in anticipation of River answering his brother's question. And now, with him touching her, it raced even more.

She took another step back from him until his hand fell completely away from her shoulder. "I'm fine," she said.

"How did you get back here?" he asked.

"Uncle Mac."

"I told him that I'd come back to get you—"

"And face the reporters?" There had been an army of them waiting outside the emergency room doors when Mac had pulled up to them. They'd gotten more photos of her, sitting in the mandatory wheelchair.

He sighed. "Guess I should have told *you* I was coming back. You thought I just dumped you there…"

She shrugged off his concerns, even while it had been what she'd thought. And it had hurt her—more than it should have.

"I'm sorry," he said. "That wasn't my intention at all. I knew the tests would take some time, and I wanted to bring Knox to take a look around here."

Knox stepped forward and held out his hand. "Edith, nice to see you again," he said.

She forced a smile for the former Ranger as she shook his hand. "So what do you think happened?"

"You tell me," he said. "You're the only one who was here."

She remembered that shadow and flinched. "I'm not so sure about that…"

"What do you remember?" Knox asked.

"I heard a clanging noise. It sounded like it was coming from here…" She glanced down at the crowbar lying on the concrete. But before she could bring up the day she'd found River down here with that, the pipes began to rattle overhead, shaking against the floor joists as water rushed through them.

Both men looked up.

"Could it have been that?" Knox asked.

"Maybe," she murmured. But the water was running now because Mac had to be in either the kitchen or the powder room. Nobody else had been in the house last night with her—at least, not that she'd seen. "I don't know…"

And she didn't know what to believe.

"What do you think?" River asked his brother. "Do you think we should call the sheriff?"

"No," Edith said. The photo of her in the ER would already bring unwanted attention to La Bonne Vie. A police report would make it so much worse. Declan would be furious. "That's not necessary."

"It is if someone's trying to hurt you," River said.

"I agree," Mac said as he joined them. "We should call the sheriff."

"And tell him what?" Edith asked. "That I overreacted to the sound of the plumbing system and knocked racks over on myself?"

"You knocked them over?" River asked, skepticism apparent in his deep voice.

She shrugged. "I was checking out the bottles on them. I could have…" She'd prefer to think it was an accident over someone actually trying to hurt her.

River ran a slightly shaking hand over his short dark hair. "I knew it—I knew I should have come back here once Thorne told me he saw you checking out of the B and B in town."

"That's why you were pacing past the window in

your apartment when I came home last night," Mac remarked. "I wondered why you were up." And it was clear that he'd been worried, probably thinking River had been having more bad dreams.

So if Mac had seen him at his ranch, the shadow Edith had glimpsed last night hadn't been River's. Hell, she wasn't even certain it had been a shadow. It could have been a lightbulb burning out that had plunged that area by the stone wall into darkness.

Edith raised her hands to quell both men's guilt. "I'm sure it was nothing," she said. "Either I bumped into one of the racks and made it unsteady or an animal tipped it over. It was just an accident. No reason for the sheriff or concern."

But she wondered, even as she said it, if she was speaking the truth or being incredibly naive. "And now that I have a clean bill of health, I need to get back to work."

"It's too soon," Uncle Mac protested. "You need to get some rest."

She smiled at her overprotective relative. "I was out all night, so I don't need to sleep any more."

"You have a concussion—"

"A slight one," she reminded him. "And I have little pain pills to pop if it bothers me at all."

"But you need to watch out for other symptoms. Nausea, dizziness—"

"And I have none of those," she assured Mac. "The only thing I am stressed over is the hours of work I have missed on this place. I have a job to do, and I need to get back to it."

River held out her phone toward her. "Yeah, your boss keeps calling."

Her pulse quickened. Had River answered the phone? Declan wouldn't be happy to have a Colton working for him. Back in foster care, she'd resented them because they'd had her uncle and she hadn't. But she'd gotten over it with time. For some reason Declan still seemed to resent them. So why had she hired River?

And why did he want to work for her? She wished he would have answered his brother. But Knox must have gotten an answer of some sort because she heard him murmur to River, "I understand…"

"What?" River echoed the question she hadn't dared ask.

"I know why you're working here," he said with a grin, and he turned toward Edith—as if she was somehow the answer. Did he think River was interested in her?

Her pulse quickened even more, and she was glad the monitors weren't on her anymore. If they'd seen her heart rate now, she probably would have been admitted instead of released.

"Nice seeing you again, Edith," Knox said and touched the brim of his hat as he walked past her. He stopped by Mac, though, and asked, "Buy you lunch?"

Mac looked at her, his eyes still so dark and serious with concern and guilt.

"I'm fine," she assured him.

But he turned to River as if looking for confirmation.

"I'll be here," River said, as if he never intended to be anywhere else.

But that wasn't possible.

He couldn't stay with her 24/7 or she would lose her mind or, worse yet, her heart.

Once it fell silent on the other side of the stone wall, the person listening to those conversations threw something at it. But the pillow made no noise, like clanging the crowbar against the rack had the night before.

How had the woman survived the accident? Those racks had looked heavy—had felt heavy—and then tumbling the crates on top of them...

But apparently Edith Beaulieu was tougher than she looked. Too bad she wasn't smart enough to quit. No job was worth her life. She would learn that soon enough, but it would be too late.

She would not escape the next *accident* as easily as she had this one.

The real question was what to do about River. He hadn't told his brother or the woman his true intention for working in the house. He'd never had any interest in La Bonne Vie, or even in his family, for that matter. He was back only because he had no place else to go.

So what was he looking for...?

And did he have any idea that the search would probably get him killed?

Chapter 10

River had kept the light off tonight so Mac wouldn't catch him pacing in front of the window. He knew he wasn't going to sleep—not with Edith alone at La Bonne Vie. So he hadn't even undressed. His boots clomped as they hit the stairs as he hurried down them to the stable. He saddled up Shadow quickly.

For once he could identify with the horse's agitation. He felt that way himself—restless, on edge...

And it wasn't because he didn't know who or what he was. He didn't give a damn about himself at the moment. He just wanted to make sure Edith was okay.

He knew she hadn't accidentally bumped into one of those racks. For the past week, he'd watched how she worked, how she moved, with the grace of a ballerina. There was no way she'd been clumsy enough to bump into anything—let alone something as large as those wine racks. As if her slight weight knocking into them could have tumbled the heavy racks over...

And the plumbing...

It wouldn't have been making any noise unless she'd been using it. Maybe she'd been running a bath or something before she'd gone downstairs. He hadn't looked into the master bathroom. There could have been a cooled tub of water in there.

But Edith was kind of like the stallion beneath him—full of nervous energy. He couldn't imagine her being able to sit in a bathtub while there was still so much work to do in the house. No. He didn't have to know her well to know that about her.

But he felt like he was beginning to know her well— well enough to know she had her suspicions about what had happened. Had she suspected him? She'd caught him with that crowbar in the wine cellar. Had she thought he was down there again when she'd heard the noise?

He cursed himself now. His damn search for answers had put her in danger. While he wanted to know the truth, he didn't want to risk her safety or anyone else's to find it.

Now he would not be able to rest until he knew she was safe. So he spurred the horse faster across Mac's fields to the fence separating the properties. Shadow cleared it easily, and instead of rattling him, the jump seemed to settle down the horse some—as if he had needed to expend some energy.

Did Edith?

Did she work so hard because she had no personal life? Or was there something more than business between her and her boss? She'd had so many missed calls from him. And that whole confidentiality agreement between them…

River realized he'd lied earlier that day. He did care who'd bought the house—but only because he cared about Edith. He wanted to know who she was working for and what the man really meant to her.

But first he wanted to make sure she was safe.

Shadow moved quickly and surefootedly across the overgrown acres of La Bonne Vie. It was as if the horse remembered the way—even in the dark.

Jade was right. The stallion was worth saving. When River had first awakened after the explosion, he'd wondered if he was worth saving. And when he'd found out he didn't even know who his father was…

He'd lost all his bearings for a while. But like Shadow, he had begun to find his way in the dark. He was healing on the outside and the inside. Helping Edith out at La Bonne Vie had proved to him that he wasn't worthless. Since he could fix that house, he could fix anything—even himself.

But it wasn't just working on the house that was healing him. It was Edith—with how she looked at him, like he was still a man. Would she look at him that way if her boss was more than just an employer to her?

Suddenly the horse reared up, pawing at the ground with his front legs. River grabbed for the pommel and gripped the horse with his legs so that he didn't fall off. Then he soothed one hand over his mane and murmured, "Easy, Shadow. It's okay."

But it wasn't. Something had definitely spooked the stallion. River peered down at the ground and also tilted his head to listen. Had the horse run across a snake? The brush was overgrown, making it hard for River—especially with only one eye—to see anything.

But Shadow wasn't looking down. He reared back and tossed his head to the left. Then River saw it, too, the shadow crouched low, moving through the brush.

Was it a coyote? A wolf? He'd heard sightings of them in the area. And the presence of a predator would certainly spook the horse.

But the predator wasn't moving toward them. It was moving toward La Bonne Vie, toward the house on the hill. River studied the shadow more closely and realized that it wasn't moving on four legs but two.

This predator was human. And it wasn't a threat to Shadow or to him but to the woman who was staying alone at La Bonne Vie.

He urged the horse forward, forcing it into a run. Maybe it was just a reporter who'd found a way around the gate. But that wasn't what River's gut was telling him. He needed to get closer, needed to stop the person before he reached the house. But suddenly the shadow vanished.

River slowed the horse down as he carefully searched the brush. The person had to be hiding. He couldn't have just disappeared.

But River could find no trace of him. Like the horse, he was spooked.

Heat climbed into Edith's face, and it wasn't because it had suddenly gotten warm in the house. In fact, it was an unseasonably cool evening in Shadow Creek. She'd shut off the air-conditioning and opened the windows. The night breeze fluttered the old, threadbare curtains in the master suite. She would need to replace those, too, like she had the mattress and the linens, before Declan came to visit.

A visit he was threatening to move up as his voice emanated from the speakers of the cell phone sitting atop the bed next to the laptop, which was open to the *Everything's Blogger* home page. "Explain those pictures to me," Declan challenged her. "Why the hell is River Colton carrying you into the ER of Shadow Creek's hospital?"

That wasn't his first question. That had been an anxious "Are you all right?"

It was only after she'd assured him that she was that he'd told her to pull up the blog. She repeated now what she'd said then. "I can't believe you even look at that tabloid crap."

"Apparently it's a good thing that I do, so I know what the hell's going on!"

He must have believed that she was really okay because anger replaced his concern now.

She flinched as her head began to pound again. Maybe she needed to take another pill to dull the pain. But she wanted to wait until she was done talking to Declan. She needed to keep her mind clear for this conversation. "It's a good thing you have such an excellent assistant that you have time to troll the internet."

He snorted, but there was amusement in it. "A good assistant would have answered her phone earlier, so I wouldn't have been so worried."

"You were?" she asked.

"Of course," he said. "You know you are far more than just an assistant to me."

The minute she'd showed up at the foster home they'd shared, Declan, older and bigger, had treated her like a little sister. She'd only been eight while he'd been sixteen. If he hadn't been so protective of her, she hated to think what might have happened. There had been a lot of angry kids in that home that might have taken out their frustrations on her. But even after Declan had left at eighteen, he'd made sure she stayed safe with frequent visits.

"I know," she said with a shaky sigh. "And I'm sorry you were worried. I didn't have my phone on me at the hospital." But she hadn't been there all day. When she'd seen the missed calls from him, she'd shot him a text saying that she was fine and would call this evening. And she'd ignored the call he'd immediately placed after that text. He had every right to be furious with her.

"I'm still worried," Declan said. "You're not acting like yourself, Edith."

She couldn't argue with him. "Maybe it's the concussion."

"Concussion!" he exclaimed, then lowered his voice as if he was worried her head was hurting. "You said you were okay."

"I am."

"If you were, you wouldn't be hanging out with a Colton. I thought you felt the same way about them that I do." And now he sounded betrayed.

"That was a long time ago," she reminded him.

Back in the foster home, she'd expressed resentment of them—that her uncle helped all of them but not her. That hadn't been fair, though, because Uncle Mac had never been given the chance to help her. Had he known what was going on, she had no doubt that he would have been there for her—like he'd been there for every one of the Coltons, even though only one child was biologically his. Thorne.

"I have never understood why you resent all of them," she admitted. Declan had treated her like a sister in every way. He'd been protective of her, but he'd also ignored her when she'd pestered him with questions.

"We were growing up in an overcrowded foster home while they were rich and entitled."

"Were," she said. They weren't anymore—at least not all of them. Certainly not River nor Thorne. "Is that why you bought this house?"

He snorted again but with nary a trace of amusement this time. "Stop changing the subject, Edith, and explain this photograph to me."

She looked at the computer screen again, and her pulse quickened with remembered excitement of being held in River's strong arms, of his chest beneath her cheek. He'd made her feel so safe and protected—more so than even Declan had ever made her feel.

But he looked fierce in the picture, his jaw tightly clenched. His hat shadowed his face, so that the patch and the scars were barely visible, but still he looked like a pirate carrying off the damsel in distress.

"Pictures can be deceiving," she reminded him. "You know that."

Like River, Declan's thick brown hair and clear green eyes and masculine bone structure made him highly photogenic. And he had been photographed with women before that had led to tabloid speculation. Was billionaire Declan Sinclair, CEO of SinCo, involved with…

Fill in the blank. There had been a couple of mod-

els, an actress and a married politician. While he might
have been dating the models and the actress, he would
have never been involved with a married woman. Hell,
Declan had never really been involved with anyone
that she knew of…

He'd always been so focused on his business. And
so had she, until now—now she couldn't stop staring
at that picture of River. He hadn't wanted to leave her
tonight. He'd been worried about her, too—like Declan.
But Declan thought River was the threat to her safety.

"Did he hurt you?" he asked. And the anger was
back.

"Of course not," she replied. "I told you—some
wine racks and crates fell over on me."

"Accidentally?" he asked suspiciously.

That shadow against the stone wall flashed through
her mind. But it could have been anything. A bulb
burning out. An animal. One of the crates moving as
it began to slide off a rack. Maybe that was what had
caused them to tip.

She had only caught a glimpse of it. And then when
she'd been hit in the head, she hadn't seen anything—
at all. She closed her eyes as the throbbing increased.

"Yes," she told Declan, even though she wasn't certain she spoke the truth.

And because he knew her so well, he called her on
the lie. "I don't feel like you're being completely honest with me, Edith."

"Now you know how I feel," she murmured.

But she'd spoken so softly, he asked, "What did
you say?"

"Nothing." He was her brother, but he was also her

boss. And as an employer, Declan tolerated no disrespect. Or dishonesty.

"How did River Colton find you?" he asked. "What the hell was he doing at La Bonne Vie?"

She flinched again. She had yet to tell him she'd hired River. It was clear that if he knew, he wouldn't be pleased. And Edith was too tired to argue at the moment.

But she was honest with him when she answered, "Declan, my head is pounding, and I really need to get some sleep."

"I'm sorry," he said. "Of course you need some rest. In fact, I should send someone else to take over for you."

She snorted now. "Like anyone else could handle this job..."

He had no idea how big it was.

"...with the discretion you want," she continued. "The reporters are relentless. They keep trespassing." She wondered now how that one had known to show up at the hospital. Had he been that shadow she'd glimpsed the night before? Had she surprised an intruder?

But River had been so certain he'd taken every necessary measure to keep them out. Nobody should have been able to get inside.

But even as she thought that, she heard it—the telltale creak of a door opening. She shivered, and it had nothing to do with the cool breeze blowing through the open windows.

"I have to go," she told Declan. And she didn't wait for his acquiescence before she clicked off her cell. She had to go. She pulled her can of pepper spray from her purse. This time she wouldn't be the one getting hurt.

* * *

In disbelief Declan stared down at the blank screen of his cell phone. Edith had just hung up on him. Not that he could blame her. She'd been hurt, and he'd been interrogating her.

But, damn it, he wanted to know what the hell River had been doing at La Bonne Vie. No Colton should have been allowed on the premises—ever again.

It wasn't theirs anymore.

It was his. He waited for the rush of satisfaction that was supposed to bring him. But he couldn't feel it.

Not yet. Maybe once he visited the house. Maybe then he would feel like it was really his and not theirs.

Would they feel that way? Would they know they'd lost everything? Like he once had?

He was no longer that pathetic poor kid he'd once been. He hadn't been for a long time—not since Edith had showed up in the foster home he'd been in. He believed it was more than coincidence that had brought her to the same foster home. Her showing up there had given him purpose.

He wasn't out for revenge just for himself but for her, too. She was too sweet and forgiving to want it for herself. So just like he'd protected her then, he would protect her now. He glanced from his blank phone screen to the monitor on his desk, and his stomach lurched as he focused on her face again, on the blood dried on her forehead and in her hair.

He wasn't doing a very damn good job of protecting her now. No matter what she'd claimed about her getting hurt in an accident, Declan believed she needed protection. The look on her face as she stared up at the man carrying her scared Declan. He hadn't been this afraid since his mother had abandoned him on that street corner in New Orleans.

He was afraid Edith was going to get hurt even worse than a concussion. He was afraid that she was going to get her heart broken.

Chapter 11

You know you are far more than just an assistant to me...

Of everything he'd overheard through the open window, that was the phrase haunting River the most. What the hell was she to her boss?

Friend?

Lover?

Dread tightened the knots that had already been in his stomach since he'd spotted that person skulking around the estate. He had to know if Edith was safe in the house alone. And he also had to know if she was romantically involved with her boss.

That was why he'd unlocked and opened the front door. But he'd barely made it across the foyer before he saw her coming down the stairwell. He couldn't remember how many times he'd watched his mom descending those stairs to make an entrance to one of her parties. She'd always worn some fancy designer gown and had her blond hair expertly styled.

Edith made more of an entrance in an old T-shirt, her long legs bare beneath the tattered hem, while her thick, dark hair hung loose around her slender shoulders. She was so damn beautiful that she took away River's breath. He could only stare at her as desire overwhelmed him.

"Who's there?" she asked, her voice cracking with fear but also with anger. She lifted a canister, pointing it toward him.

He realized he was standing in the shadows, so he stepped into the light. "It's me."

She dropped the can and pressed a hand over her heart. With the thin fabric tight against her chest, he could tell she wore no bra beneath it. Her nipples were taut beneath the cotton. "You scared me!" she said.

He picked up the can, which had rolled down the steps to land next to his boot. Still leaning over, he peered up at her. She remained a few steps up but not high enough that he could see beneath the T-shirt.

Was she completely naked beneath it?

His heart raced at the thought. "I'm sorry," he said as he straightened up and handed the can back to her.

"What are you doing back here?" she asked, and her fingers trembled as she took the can from him. "I told you I'd be fine alone."

"Are you alone?" he asked. He'd assumed he'd overheard another phone call between her and her boss. But the T-shirt she wore was so big it clearly belonged to a man. Maybe that man was in the house, in her bed.

Her hair looked mussed. Maybe someone had been running his hands through it, like River wanted to run his.

Her brow furrowed slightly. "Of course I'm alone."

"I thought I heard a man's voice," he explained.

"Oh." She sighed. "I had my boss on speaker. What did you overhear?"

"Enough to know he doesn't like me or my family," he admitted to eavesdropping. "Why doesn't he?"

She shrugged. "I don't know." Then her dark eyes narrowed. "Maybe it's because you don't listen. You didn't need to come back here."

"Yeah, I did," he said as he remembered his reason for being there. "I saw someone heading toward the house."

She glanced beyond him toward the driveway. "The gate's been keeping everyone out. Nobody's driven up. Not even you."

"I rode," he said. "I was out for a ride when I noticed someone heading across the fields toward the house."

She shivered. "Are you sure it was a person?"

He was beginning to worry that they'd blamed too much on four-legged animals. The noises in the house. The racks and crates being knocked over onto her. "Absolutely certain."

"Did you catch him?" she asked.

He shook his head.

"Then how can you be certain? You were out in the fields where it's dark."

"I know it was human."

"Then how could it outrun your horse?" she asked.

River tensed. "I don't know. It just all of a sudden disappeared." Kind of like it had dropped down a rabbit hole. But if he told her that, she would insist it was a rabbit he'd seen.

She tilted her head as if she doubted his story.

"I saw something," he insisted. Sure, his eyesight wasn't what it had once been. But he knew that had been a person he and Shadow had seen heading toward the house.

"Yes, you did," she agreed. "An excuse to come up and check on me."

He couldn't deny it. "I am worried about you," he admitted. "I can't stop thinking about how you spent the entire night last night lying on the concrete—hurt, cold, alone…"

If she had actually been alone…

Or had someone else been inside the house with her? Had someone knocked over those racks and crates on purpose, wanting to hurt her?

She shivered. He wasn't sure if she was cold now or if she was chilled from remembering her ordeal. But then she shrugged off his concern and murmured, "It's not the first time."

And he remembered she'd been through far worse ordeals than last night—with her mother. "Edith…"

She held up her hands as if to ward off his concern. "I'm fine," she assured him. "I'm tough."

He had no doubt about that. "I know."

"But you're still worried."

He nodded. "Will you at least let me check the house? Make sure that no one else is inside? Or aren't I allowed in here anymore?"

"How much of my conversation did you overhear?" she asked.

"The window was open, and you had the phone on speaker," he reminded her.

She groaned. "You weren't supposed to hear any of that."

"Why does your boss hate all the Coltons?" It must have been why he'd bought the house—for some twisted sense of revenge.

She didn't try denying it, just shrugged and replied, "I don't know."

From what he'd overheard, he knew she spoke the truth. "He accused you of not being completely honest with him, but it sounds like he's the one keeping secrets from you."

She sighed. "He wasn't wrong. I haven't been completely honest with him," she admitted, her voice heavy with regret. "I didn't tell him you're working here."

He stepped closer to her. With her up a couple steps, she was the same height as he was now. "Why not?"

"You know," she said.

He shook his head.

"You overheard enough to realize that he'd make me fire you."

"Oh, I know that," he heartily agreed. "What I don't know is why you wouldn't want to fire me." Was it possible—could she be as attracted to him as he was to her? He'd caught her glances whenever he went without a shirt. Had he just imagined her interest?

She gestured around the dimly lit foyer. "You've done a lot of work around here."

He'd worked his ass off to impress her—all the while he should have been searching the house for his mother's secret rooms. "Yeah, I got it ready for your boss's visit."

Just one bedroom, though, and she'd moved into that. Did she intend to share it with him?

"So do you want me to fire you?" she asked.

"No." And it wasn't just because he still wanted to

search for those rooms. It was because of her—because he wanted to keep spending his days with her. "I told you that I need this job."

"You don't need this job," she said, as her dark eyes narrowed slightly with suspicion. "With your skills, you can do anything you want to do."

"Really?" he asked.

"Yes," she said. "Your injury is not holding you back at all."

It was, though. If he didn't have the scars and the missing eye, he might have done what he wanted to do sooner. "So you really think I can do anything I want?"

She sighed slightly, as if she was getting annoyed with him. "Yes, I do."

So he reached up and slid one arm around her waist to draw her tightly against him. Then he cupped the back of her head in his free hand and lowered her face to his.

And he kissed her.

Her lips were as silky as her skin and her hair. He brushed his softly across them.

She gasped, and her breath whispered across his skin. Her palms against his chest, she pushed him back but not completely away. His arm was still looped around her waist. "What are you doing?" she asked.

"You told me I can do anything I want," he reminded her, and his voice was gruff with the desire overwhelming him. "This is what I want to do—what I've wanted to do for a long time." Ever since that first night he'd heard her scream and found her in the basement with her pepper spray and indomitable spirit.

Her lips curved into a slight smile. "I didn't mean this…"

But she didn't protest when he tugged her back against him and kissed her again. Instead she kissed him, too, her lips moving against his, parting as her tongue slipped out and into his mouth.

He groaned as passion rushed over him, tensing every muscle in his body. He poured that passion into his kiss, making love to her mouth like he wanted to make love to her body. His hands moved, one through her hair—the other from her slender waist over the slight curve of her hip to her bare thigh. The muscle was toned, while her skin was smooth and silky. He brushed his fingertip over it—then moved his hand up, beneath the T-shirt. He had to know what she wore beneath it—if anything.

His heart pounded hard against his ribs—as he waited for her to stop him. But she only emitted a soft moan as he nibbled at her bottom lip. Then he slid his hand up her thigh, over the curve of her butt. She wasn't completely naked. A thin piece of lace covered her. He was tempted to tear it aside and just take her there—on the stairs.

But he lifted her—not like he had from the basement floor. He didn't cradle her in his arms. Instead he lifted her, so that her legs wrapped around his waist and the heat of her core pressed against the erection straining the fly of his jeans. He groaned. But she swallowed it in her mouth as she kissed him deeply.

His legs shook a little as want turned to need. But he began to climb the stairs up to the bedroom. Now he wanted more than a kiss from her—so much more...

The last time River Colton had carried her, she'd had a concussion. So she'd had an excuse for feeling light-headed and out of control. She had no excuse now.

But desire.

It heated her skin, had blood rushing through her veins, her heart pounding...

As he climbed the stairs, she moved up and down, her core rubbing against his erection. She ached for him to fill her, to fill the emptiness she hadn't ever felt as acutely as she did now.

He groaned as she moved. Cords strained along his neck and muscles bulged in his shoulders. She knew he wasn't straining from carrying her. She'd watched him carry even heavier things over the past week he'd worked for her. He wanted her every bit as much as she wanted him.

But he worked for her—at least until Declan found out. And Edith had never mixed business with pleasure before. She knew it would be incredible, incomparable pleasure to make love with River. Just his kiss had made her feel more passion than she ever had before. The way his mouth moved over hers...

He kissed her again—even as he climbed the stairs. He must have instinctively known where he was going since there was no way he could see, not with his face pressed to hers. But he made it to the top of the stairwell and walked unerringly down the hall to the open double doors to the master suite.

As he lowered her onto the bed, she reached up and ran her fingers down his handsome face. Her fingertips brushed over the hard ridge of the scar along his right cheek, near the patch. And he tensed.

"Does it hurt?" she asked.

He settled her onto the mattress, but he didn't follow her down onto it. Instead he pulled back—as if he couldn't handle her touching his face.

He shook his head. "No…"

But it must have. She could see the pain on his face; it stood out more than the scar. "But it haunts you," she said, remembering that morning she'd heard him yelling.

He shrugged, but there was nothing nonchalant about it. His shoulders moved slowly, as if a heavy burden was always across them. "We all have things in our past that stay with us. Sounds like you do, too."

"You heard," she said and tried to remember what all she and Declan had discussed. "You know I lived in a foster home for a while."

He nodded. "Because your mother couldn't take care of you."

"She couldn't take care of herself, either. Especially after my father died." Edith had loved her father and missed him. But she had never seen anyone in as much pain as her mother had suffered over the loss of her husband.

So when River reached out for her, she drew back, scooting up to lean against the headboard. This man had already made her feel things she hadn't felt before— a passion and desire she hadn't even realized she was capable of feeling. She couldn't risk going any further with him, not when she was worried she might get sick.

"I'm sorry," he said.

She didn't know if he was apologizing for what had happened with her mom or for kissing her. She didn't want his apology or his pity or whatever he was giving her.

She shook her head. "We can't do this," she said.

"I can," he said.

"I can't." The risk was too great.

"Why not?" he asked. "You must feel it, too—this attraction between us…"

She'd felt it the first time she'd seen him. But she'd refused to acknowledge it then. And now she intended to ignore it. "No."

He blew out a ragged breath. "Well, I guess your boss isn't the only one you're not being completely open and honest with." He glanced down at where her cell phone sat next to her laptop on the bed. "Is this about him?"

Declan obviously wouldn't be happy. But he had no say in her love life. Of course there had never been much reason for him to have a say. She had only ever dated sporadically. A couple of boys in high school, a couple in college—a few more dates since graduation.

They had never gone much beyond that, though. She had never been tempted to fall for any of them. Still, none of them had ever made her feel like River just had—so out of control and desperate with desire.

"This is about me," she said. "I can't risk…" Her heart. Her sanity. She wasn't certain which risk posed a greater threat.

He nodded as if he suddenly understood. And he stood. "I understand…"

She doubted that when she wasn't certain she understood herself. "You do?"

He touched his face where her fingertips had brushed over the scar. "It's this…"

"What?"

"This injury."

The scar did nothing to detract from his handsomeness. Nor did the patch. In fact, it gave him a look of danger, which made him even sexier.

"You're worried," he continued, "that it messed me up like your mom. That I have PTSD."

She sucked in a breath. But she couldn't deny that she'd wondered. "Do you?"

He shrugged. "I don't know. I haven't had another nightmare since that morning you heard me." His mouth curved up slightly. "Maybe you've healed me."

Panic gripped her, stealing away her breath as a pressure settled heavily on her chest. That was how she'd felt with her mother—that she could somehow heal her. But no matter how hard she'd tried, she had always failed to help her.

Even now, with Declan helping her pay for her mother's treatment; she visited as often as she was able. Mom hadn't recognized her for years, though.

"No," she murmured. "I can't…"

She hadn't helped Merrilee. She wouldn't be able to help River. But most of all, she was afraid that if she fell for him, she wouldn't be able to help herself.

"I can't do this," she said again.

He didn't argue with her. He just walked away. It was a while before she heard the front door close behind him. He must have searched the house like he'd asked—to make certain that she was alone.

For the first time ever at La Bonne Vie, she actually felt alone. Completely alone.

"You're worried."

Mac sighed. But he couldn't argue with his son's assessment. He was worried. "Yes."

"About who?" Thorne asked as he settled into one of the wicker chairs on the front porch of his father's ranch house. "Edith?"

"Yes," Mac replied.

"You don't think that stuff falling on her in the wine cellar was an accident?" Thorne asked.

"Where'd you hear about all that?" Mac asked. He hadn't spoken to his son yet that day. Thorne had been working on his house, trying to get it finished before his and Maggie's child came into the world.

Mac's grandchild. Pride filled his heart. But he already had another grandson in Knox's boy. Knox was like his son, Cody like his grandson. Maybe Maggie would have a girl. But then she would probably remind him of Edith and all the ways he'd failed his niece.

"Knox," Thorne said. "He came by the house to talk to Allison and filled me in. Why didn't you call?"

"Thought you'd see it on *Everything's Blogger in Texas*," Mac said, remembering how the reporters had hounded him and Edith as they'd left the hospital.

"Maybe the site knows what the hell's going on at La Bonne Vie," Thorne said. "Edith won't say anything."

"Damn confidentiality agreement," Mac remarked. He wondered who her boss was and why he was so determined to protect his privacy. "People that bent on secrecy must have a hell of a lot to hide." Like Livia and all those damn secret rooms she'd had in La Bonne Vie.

He shivered, wishing he'd dressed warmer. But he hadn't been cold until he'd left Evelyn and returned home to find the place all quiet and dark—even the room above the stables. He must have looked in that direction because Thorne did, too.

"Is he asleep or gone?"

"Gone," Mac replied. "I don't think he sleeps. But I can't blame him, not with the way he wakes up shouting…"

"He's not getting any better?" Thorne asked.

Mac paused to think and consider. "Actually he has been better since he's been working on La Bonne Vie. Maybe the hard work has settled some of his restlessness."

"It's not restlessness," Thorne said. "He probably has PTSD. He needs to talk to someone."

"I don't think we should push him." He was doing better—much better since Edith had put him to work. But was that because of the work or Edith?

"Do you want him winding up like Aunt Merrilee?" Thorne asked.

Mac flinched with guilt over how he'd failed his sister. He never should have lost touch with her. When she'd stopped taking his calls and had returned his letters unopened, he should have tracked her and Edith down to make certain they were all right. Then he flinched when he heard the whinny of the horse and realized River had ridden up. He hoped the young man hadn't overheard them.

But his hopes were dashed when River said, "So you both think I have PTSD, too?"

"Too?" Thorne asked as he stood and turned to lean over the porch railing.

"I'm sorry," Mac said. "We didn't realize you were…"

River slid off the horse's back and dropped to the ground. "It's fine. Not the first time I eavesdropped tonight and heard something I didn't want to."

"What?" Thorne asked him. "What's going on up at La Bonne Vie?"

"Absolutely nothing," River replied with a trace of bitterness.

"Did she fire you?" Mac asked. He wouldn't have

put it past his niece to do just that if River had tried to protect her. And he had no doubt that the ex-Marine had gone up there to make sure she was okay.

River cared about the young woman—maybe nearly as much as Mac did. But in the nine years since she'd left the foster home and reached out to him, Mac had gotten to know her pretty well. He knew how fiercely independent she was.

River hesitated for a long moment, as if he wasn't certain himself whether or not he was still employed. "Not yet…"

What the hell had gone on between them?

Thorne narrowed his eyes and flat out asked, "What happened?"

"That other conversation I overheard," River said. "Let's just say her boss didn't buy that place because he loves Coltons…"

Thorne sighed. And Mac felt a fresh wave of guilt. He hated what his son and the other Colton kids had had to endure because of their mother. He had never been able to help anyone he cared about as much as he wished he could have.

"And I don't think Edith has very warm, fuzzy feelings about us, either," River continued.

Mac didn't believe that. He knew Edith loved her cousin Thorne. And he'd seen the way she looked at River—even the way she'd looked for him at the hospital when Mac had showed up in his place. He suspected she had very warm, fuzzy feelings for River. And that was the problem. At least for her.

And unfortunately for River, as well—because she would push him away as far as she could. It probably was only a matter of time before she fired him. But River appeared to realize that already.

"Is she safe up there?" Thorne asked. That must have been why he'd stopped over—to ask Mac the same thing. But River had been there.

River nodded. "Yeah. I checked out the house again. There was no sign of anyone else being in there but her. And if there was…"

"What?" Thorne asked.

"I don't think Edith would have any problem getting rid of them." Without another word, he tugged the horse's reins, leading him off toward the barn.

"What the hell's wrong with him?" Thorne asked.

Mac shrugged. Was it a bruised ego? Pride or heart? Was River falling for Edith?

Chapter 12

River pulled his hat low over his face as he hurried down the sidewalk of Main Street. He hated coming to town, but he'd been called to this meeting. Unfortunately, it was being held in his sister's boutique. As if he wasn't conspicuous enough with this patch and his scar, now they had him walking into a women's clothing shop.

Hoping no damn reporter spied him, he hurried through the door and ducked low behind the racks of clothes. "He's in the back," Evelyn called to him with a smile from the antique-looking cash register at the vintage-style front counter.

The place was fancy and European-looking—just like his sister Claudia had always been. After what she'd learned, River had no right to feel sorry for himself. Claudia had learned neither of her parents were who she'd always thought they were. She wasn't even a Colton.

But then, that wasn't necessarily a bad thing. She must have been out and about somewhere or her effervescent personality would have been overflowing the boutique.

He pushed open the door marked Employees Only and stepped into the back office. Their oldest sister, Leonor, Claudia's business partner, wasn't there, either. It was Leonor's fiancé, Joshua Howard, who sat at the cluttered desk in the back. Designs and fashion magazines covered the surface. River couldn't imagine the former FBI agent had been looking at any of it.

"You wanted to meet here?" River asked incredulously.

Josh grinned. "Figured you'd prefer here to the local coffee shop."

"Where people gawk and stare and, if any reporters are around, take photos?" River shuddered. "Thanks. I do." Not that he didn't feel awkward in the boutique, too.

Josh didn't look particularly comfortable, either, on the dainty chair with the spindly legs. But he stretched out his long legs and braced an elbow on the desk. "I'm here because I'm figuring out what kind of security system Claudia should install in the boutique," he explained.

That explained why Josh was there. But why had he called River to meet him? "That's good…" He was sure they could use one.

"I have my business just about up and running in Austin," Josh said.

"The security business?" Josh had retired from the

FBI to be his own boss. Of course the Bureau might not have given him much choice in the matter once he'd fallen for the daughter of one of their most wanted fugitives.

Josh nodded.

"Good for you," River said, even as he wondered if it was good for the Coltons. Having a man on the inside of the FBI had been helpful. Josh had been the one who'd found out River was alive and okay and had assured the others. He'd also kept them apprised of all the Livia sightings. But River shoved aside his selfishness and held out his hand. "Congratulations."

"Thanks," Josh said as he shook. "So you want a job?"

River snorted. "What?"

"Working security with me," Josh said. "You want a job?"

Security. He knew a lot of ex-Marines who'd gone into the business. Several guys from another unit had recently become bodyguards at the Payne Protection Agency in Michigan. He was intrigued. "You don't think I'm damaged goods like everyone else?"

"I know what you did over there," Josh said. "I have buddies in the Corps." In high places, obviously, since he'd found out more about River's last mission than any civilian was supposed to know.

"Yeah, that's why I'm asking you," River said. "You don't think I'm all screwed up with PTSD?"

"Are you?" Josh asked.

River sighed. "I have a nightmare every now and then but they're getting fewer and far between." Because now he dreamed about Edith, about her lips, her skin, her long sexy legs…and that was only if his tense, achy body let him sleep at all.

Josh said, "I know you got help right away—right after the mission. You didn't try to go it alone."

He'd wanted to be well before he returned to his family. But no matter how hard he'd tried, he'd not been able to completely heal either the external or the internal scars before he'd returned.

While he'd talked to someone, being alone had probably been the best medicine for him. Working the ranch, riding.

But he hadn't felt whole again until he'd met Edith. She'd brought out feelings in him he hadn't felt for a while—protectiveness and desire.

"No, I haven't gone it alone," River agreed. But he was thinking about her—not the Corps' shrink. After what she'd gone through with her mom, she didn't think she could help anyone, but she had already helped him.

"So come to work with me," Josh urged him.

River was tempted. But the thought of leaving La Bonne Vie...

Of leaving Edith...

"I have a job right now," he said. But he doubted that would last. Edith hadn't fired him last night, but he had no doubt that she would—once her boss showed up for his visit. So River didn't have much time left to find all of Livia's secret rooms and secret records.

"Yeah, Knox told me you're working at the estate."

"Did you offer him a job, too?" River asked.

Josh shook his head. "I think there's a better job out there for Knox."

"Sheriff of Shadow Creek?" The one they had was an ineffectual joke, and they'd all been encouraging Knox to run for the office.

"He told me about your strange feelings around La

Bonne Vie—like someone might be hanging around there."

River's blood chilled as he realized who Josh was thinking the intruder might be. He shook his head. "No…she wouldn't risk coming back here."

"She already has," Josh reminded him. They were all pretty certain she'd killed her grandson's kidnapper and had visited Leonor in the hospital after her half brother had tried to kill her. He had wound up as dead as the kidnapper. So every time she'd returned someone else had died. If she was back, who would it be this time?

River glanced at his watch. "I better get to the job I do have now." And make sure that Edith was safe.

"Whenever you decide you want it, the security job is all yours," Josh assured him. "Just make sure you stay alive to take it."

River tensed. "You don't think my mother would actually hurt one of her own children?"

"Leonor doesn't," Josh said. But he obviously didn't share his fiancée's faith in his mother-in-law-to-be. "But you and I are more aware of what people are capable of—especially when they're cornered and desperate."

Anything. They were capable of anything at that point. But River wasn't worried about himself. He was worried about Edith. He didn't care who saw him as he hurried out of the boutique and back to his truck—and back to La Bonne Vie.

Edith moved slowly around the house, and not just because she was still a little achy from getting flattened onto the concrete a couple nights ago. Guilt weighed heavily on her over how she'd treated River the night before. She had let him kiss her and touch her and then she'd gotten scared and had freaked out on him. He'd left thinking she'd rejected him because of him—because of his injury and his possible PTSD.

But she'd been more afraid of her own mental state than his. She was afraid of falling—like her mother had—so far and so deep that she wouldn't be able to function without the man. And maybe her fears were founded because for the first time she felt like she couldn't function—and it was all because River hadn't showed up for work yet.

Was he going to?

Had he taken her rejection so personally that he'd quit? But if he'd been that upset last night, why would he have checked the house to make sure it was safe, that she was safe? Why wouldn't he have said that he wasn't coming back?

She gasped as a horrible thought occurred to her. What if he'd been hurt on his way back to Uncle Mac's ranch? He'd seen someone in the fields. What if that someone had just been hiding and waiting for him to circle back to Mac's?

As that burden of guilt she'd been carrying grew even heavier, she nearly dropped the vase she was holding. Here she'd been working on the damn inventory while River could be lying out in the fields somewhere, hurt.

Or even worse...

She needed to call Uncle Mac and see if he had returned to the ranch last night. Or better yet, she needed to go find River herself—to make sure he was all right.

Like he had checked on her last night. And she'd rewarded his chivalry by making him feel bad.

Tears of regret stung her eyes. And as she blinked them away, she noticed movement in the foyer—a shadow blocking out the sunshine. She dropped the vase, which shattered onto the marble floor.

"Are you all right?" River asked as he rushed toward her.

Shards of the porcelain had come quite close to her bare toes. Since she'd been working on inventory, she was wearing flip-flops, shorts and a tank top. Fortunately it had just been a cheap florist's vase from a display that had dried out years ago. "Yes," she replied. "You startled me."

"I'm sorry," he said. "I should have knocked—"

"No, it's all right," she said. And it was now that she knew he was all right. "I was worrying about you."

"About me?" he asked. Then his brow lowered, and he groaned. "You don't need to worry about me. I'm fine—really."

"I was worried you weren't coming back," she admitted.

He stared at her for a moment, his left eye narrowed as he studied her face. Did he see how worried she'd been? How much she regretted turning him away the night before?

She'd lain awake, aching with that emptiness she knew he would have been able to fill. She'd been able to taste him yet on her lips and to feel his hands on her. And her body had pulsed with need.

She closed her eyes, so he wouldn't see that need— that hunger. That feeling—that desperate desire—was why she couldn't get involved with him. She was safer with the other men she'd dated, the ones who hadn't inspired any deep emotion in her. She was more comfortable with that; she felt safer.

He chuckled. "I must be more used to rejection than the other guys you've turned down," he told her. "You just stung my pride a little."

She opened her eyes to study his face now. She suspected he was downplaying how he'd really felt. She'd hurt more than his pride the night before. "I went farther than just saying no," she said, "and that was uncalled for. I'm sorry."

His broad shoulders moved up and down in a quick shrug. "It's fine. I get it. You're not interested."

But she was. She was more interested than she'd ever been before. But she couldn't admit that now. He might reach for her again. He might kiss her.

Then she opened her mouth because she wanted him to touch her, to kiss her...

But he reached for a broom instead and began sweeping up the shards of the vase she'd dropped. "You seem a little rattled," he remarked. "Had you been hearing anything else before I showed up?"

"What do you mean?" she asked.

"Any of those weird noises again?" he asked. "Like the clanging or the creaking?"

She shook her head. She almost wished she would have. It would have distracted her from thinking about him, from obsessing about him, about how passionately he'd kissed her, about how he'd carried her up those stairs...

"Did you have that feeling today that you're not alone?" he asked.

She bristled slightly at all the questions. "Do you think I'm seeing things?"

He shook his head. "No. I don't. I've seen things around here, too," he reminded her. "Like that person on the grounds last night."

She shivered. "Are you trying to scare me now?" She'd convinced herself, and Declan, that it had just been an accident. Otherwise Declan probably would have hired security for the estate.

"Not at all, but I think you're spending too much time here," he said. "You got hurt the other night and came right back to work. You need to take a break. You need to get out of this house."

"Why do I feel like you're trying to get rid of me?"

He shook his head. "Not at all. I just want you to take a break for a change. We have that dinner tonight, too."

"Dinner tonight?" she asked.

"At Mac's," he replied like he thought she knew. "He and Evelyn are cooking. Thorne and Maggie will be there, as well. Maybe even Claudia and Hawk."

"Oh," she said. "It's a family dinner."

He shrugged. "I guess."

"I wasn't invited."

He snorted. "Of course you were."

She shook her head.

"You're family."

She shrugged. "I'm not a Colton."

"That makes you damn lucky," he said. "But you're coming, anyway." He stepped closer to her, and his one-eyed gaze dipped to her mouth. "As my date."

"River..."

"I know, I know, you're not interested in a hot mess

like me," he assured her, but he did it with a grin, as if she hadn't hurt him the night before. "But you need to come as my date, so that I'm not third-wheeling or fifth- or seventh-wheeling—whatever the hell it would be." He shuddered. "I'm so sick of doing that."

"But won't we give everyone the wrong impression?" she asked. Though it was herself she was worried about—that she might believe he was her date.

"Do you really care what everyone else thinks?"

"I'm your boss," she reminded him, and herself.

"And you never socialize with *your* boss?" he asked. All the teasing was gone now. He looked serious and very interested in her reply.

Did he think she and Declan had more than a professional relationship? They did. They were family.

But Declan didn't even want anyone to know she worked for him, so he undoubtedly didn't want them to know they were foster siblings.

"We socialize," she replied.

A muscle twitched along his tightly clenched jaw, and he nodded. "Okay, then, it's settled. If you can socialize with him, you can socialize with me. After all, we're family."

But they were not related in any way, nor did she have any sisterly feelings toward him like she had with Declan. She wished she had—then she wouldn't be so damn attracted to him. Being alone with him so much wasn't helping, either, especially now after last night, after how they'd nearly made love.

While earlier she'd been worried about him because he hadn't showed up yet, now she was worried because he had. She was worried about herself. Her lips tingled for his kisses. And her body heated as desire pumped through it with her blood. She couldn't work near him as she had been doing.

If he took off his shirt again…

Her heart began to pound fast and almost violently. No. She couldn't stay here with him. Sure, she could probably find some project for him to do outside. But she knew she would wind up watching him through the windows, like she had before.

She needed some distance from him. And maybe that would help her regain her perspective. Maybe this attraction was only due to proximity.

"Okay," she said. "I'll go with you tonight." With that many other people around, she wouldn't be alone with him. She wouldn't even have to be close to him.

"Should we bring anything to it?" he asked.

He'd inadvertently given her the perfect excuse. "We should bring something," she agreed. "I'll go into town and pick up a bottle of wine." She was already heading up the stairs to change her clothes. "Or maybe some ingredients to make an appetizer or dessert…"

Just moments later she was changed and ready to leave, but she hesitated at the door and turned back to him. He looked expectant, like he was just waiting for her to go. Waiting for what?

And had he inadvertently given her the excuse to leave or had he been trying to get rid of her?

"Take your time," he urged her. "I'll just finish up a few projects around here, then go home and clean up for dinner."

She nodded in agreement. But she felt strange leaving him alone in the house.

She had that feeling all over again—like there was

something else going on with River Colton, something he didn't want her to know.

The woman was gone. For the moment...

She would, no doubt, return—for whatever purpose she served at La Bonne Vie. Inventory?

Inventory of what? There was nothing left of value in the house, at least not where anyone would be able to find it. Except maybe him...

River had not left. In fact, the moment the woman's car had pulled away from the house, he'd come down to the basement. And the clanging of the crowbar and scraping of its end against the stone wall of the wine cellar forewarned how close he was.

Too close...

Metal cracked as the lock snapped. Then hinges creaked as the stone door swung open into the secret chamber. Except that it was no longer secret.

River had found it.

A shaking hand reached for the gun sitting atop the bureau. It would have been better if the woman had found the room. Killing her would have been easy.

Killing River wouldn't be easy. But if he continued his search, it would prove necessary.

Chapter 13

River reeled back at the blast...of the damp, musty air escaping through the door he'd just opened.

"What the hell..." he murmured as he stepped inside the small space. It looked like just another part of the wine cellar, complete with racks and crates. But there were still bottles on the shelves here. He reached out to inspect one, but there was too much dust on the label.

He didn't know anything about wine, but he suspected this was where his mother had kept the most valuable vintages. He would have thought she'd have left them out on display. But maybe she hadn't legally acquired them—like so much else in her life. Like Claudia...

Edith would be happy about this discovery.

If he told her.

How could he tell her without revealing that he'd

been snooping around the basement? She would fire him for certain if she knew what his true motivation for working for her was.

It was no longer his only motivation, though. She motivated him—more than anything or anyone else ever had. But she already worried about him, and probably not just because of his possibly having PTSD.

His mother was a cold-blooded killer.

He needed to know who his father was—needed to know if he was like Livia or like Mac or like Jade's dad…

So River searched beyond the racks and crates. But there were no records hidden in there. There was another suspicious-looking wall, though.

Was there another room beyond it? Did each room open onto another? Was the entire basement a maze of secret rooms, maybe secret tunnels?

His heart began to race with anticipation. If his mother had gone to so much trouble to create so many hiding spaces, she must have hidden plenty down there. Like his paternity.

He picked up the crowbar and started on the new door. Knowing now where he'd found the last latch, it was easier to find this one. The next door popped open more easily, and when it scraped across the concrete floor, it didn't disturb a bed of dust like the last one had.

Nor did he feel a blast of damp, stale air. This room wasn't as closed up as the last one had been. Nor was it as empty…

He tightened his grasp on the crowbar. But he really wished he had a gun—because he almost thought he heard the telltale click of one cocking. And if he had, he would have no place to hide before the trigger was pulled...

Edith hadn't noticed the shop on Main Street before. She must have driven straight past it when she'd been staying in town.

But how could she have missed it? With its brick painted white and its rich caramel-colored trim, it stood out from the darker brick buildings on either side of it. A sign hanging between the first and second stories proclaimed it the Honeysuckle Road.

Her trip to town had been for wine or food to bring to the dinner party. No. Her trip to town had been to avoid spending any more time alone with River Colton.

So she might as well spend some time checking out the new boutique. After parking her car down the street, she headed back to the newly white-washed building and pushed open the door. A bell tinkled, announcing her arrival.

The woman behind the counter glanced up and offered a welcoming smile. She was a petite, black woman who looked vaguely familiar to Edith. Her smile widened with recognition, and her dark eyes sparkled. "Edith," she exclaimed as she stepped out from behind the counter and approached her. "I'm so glad you stopped by to visit."

"I..." *Am at a loss.* River had her so rattled that she couldn't immediately place the other woman.

"Evelyn," the woman reminded her. "I'm your Uncle Mac's girlfriend." Evelyn chuckled. "But I haven't been a girl for a while." Her skin was so smooth and flawless, she looked closer to Edith's twenty-seven years than Mac's fifty-six, though.

"You're a hottie and you know it or Mac wouldn't be so crazy about you," teased another woman who stepped out from behind a rack where she'd been hanging clothes. She was tall with ample curves and long, straight blond hair. Her gray eyes lit up when she saw Edith. She rushed forward and enveloped her in a hug, saying, "I'm so glad you came to visit."

The young woman was such a force of nature that there was no forgetting Claudia Colton—especially with as much as she'd been in the news lately. It had just recently been discovered that she wasn't even a Colton. But that was probably not a bad thing.

Honeysuckle Road...

Of course this was Claudia's shop. She'd opened it up with the help of her sister Leonor, and she featured her own designs in it.

"I should have come sooner to check it out," Edith said as she hugged her back. Claudia had designed a gorgeous wedding gown for Thorne's bride. Edith couldn't wait to check out the racks of clothes filling the shop.

Claudia laughed. "Not sure we have something small enough for you here."

"Do you have anything big enough for me?" another voice chimed in, along with the bell announcing her arrival in the shop. "I've already outgrown the maternity clothes you've already made me." Maggie Colton ran a hand over her protruding belly. Her blue eyes sparkled with happiness. Like Claudia, she pulled Edith into a hug.

Edith gasped as she felt the baby move between them.

"Yeah, he's a kicker," Maggie said as she rubbed her belly again.

"He?" Edith asked.

Maggie shrugged. "I don't know for certain."

"Hope it's a girl," Claudia said. "I've already started designing some dresses for her."

"Of course you have," Maggie said.

"And I have some more maternity clothes that I think you'll love," Claudia promised her.

"She also has some things you'll love," Evelyn assured Edith. "Honeysuckle Road carries all sizes. Mac said you're a runner."

"Yes." And it was sort of an addiction for her. If she didn't get in a good run, she got too stressed out and restless. Maybe that was what was wrong with her. Because of the concussion, she hadn't been able to run yet. It wasn't that she wanted to have sex with River; it was that she needed to log some miles.

Her body pulsed at just the thought of River, of him touching her. And she knew a run wouldn't be enough to help her overcome her attraction to him.

"We'll find you something, too," Claudia assured her.

"I'm glad you came by," Evelyn said. "Mac texted me earlier that he hadn't had the chance to ask you to dinner yet. Now I can."

"River already invited me," she said. All of the women turned toward her, speculation in their gazes as they stared at her. Heat rushed to her face. "Not like that…"

"Like what?" Claudia asked, her lips curving into a slight smile.

"It's not a date," Edith insisted. "It's just a family

dinner." She instantly regretted saying that, but Claudia had no reaction. Even though she had no Colton DNA, she must have still considered herself one.

"Technically," Maggie said. "You're only related to Mac and Thorne—not River."

"That's true," Claudia remarked, her gray eyes twinkling.

Evelyn leaned closer and whispered, "Watch out for that matchmaker."

"Do you have any complaints?" Claudia teased her.

Evelyn smiled and waved a hand in front of her face, as if it had suddenly gotten hot in the boutique. "None at all."

Edith's heart filled with happiness for her uncle. After all Livia Colton had put him through, he deserved it. And Evelyn seemed like such a lovely woman.

"What about you?" Claudia turned to Edith.

"About what?" she asked. "I'm very happy for my uncle and Evelyn."

"No," Claudia said. "About River. Do you have any complaints?"

"We're not dating," Edith repeated. "He's working for me."

"At La Bonne Vie," Claudia murmured with a grimace of revulsion. "I can't believe he's willingly hanging out there. But then, River hasn't been himself since he's come back."

"Who is he, then?" Edith asked.

And the chatty Claudia fell suddenly silent. After a long moment, she replied, "I guess I don't know anymore. He was gone for ten years, with just a few short visits home between deployments."

"Mac said that he was just a boy when he enlisted and left for the Marines," Evelyn added.

"Then he came back a man," Edith found herself remarking. More man than she'd ever met before. He was so strong—so masculine. Her pulse quickened just thinking about him.

Claudia looked at her again with that gleam of speculation in her eyes. And Edith could have bitten off her tongue for her slip.

"Is he all right?" Maggie asked. "Thorne is very worried about him."

Edith remembered that first morning after her return to Shadow Creek when she'd heard River calling out in his sleep. He had been caught up in a nightmare that morning. But he'd quickly awakened from it and shaken off the vestiges of whatever horrors he'd endured during his deployments. And she had seen no signs since that he struggled with either emotional or physical wounds.

He was ostensibly recovered. So she'd had no right to question him the night before. But she'd been desperate then to protect herself from the feelings he'd inspired in her.

She shrugged, but she couldn't shake off the memories of his kisses, of his touch…

"I don't know what he was like before," she replied. "But he seems fine. He's been working very hard to help get La Bonne Vie ready."

"Ready for what?" Claudia asked. "What does your boss intend to do with it?"

Edith shrugged again and turned her attention to the racks of brightly colored clothes. After the destruction and drabness of La Bonne Vie, she needed vibrancy.

And maybe—just maybe—she wanted to look good tonight.

"She can't talk about it," Evelyn answered for her. "Her boss has her locked into a confidentiality agreement." Mac must have shared Edith's situation with her, and she'd sweetly jumped to her defense. Just like River had with Jade.

He had defended her to his own family.

The petite woman turned toward Claudia with a grin. "Maybe we should think about having one of those."

"So you can't talk about me?" Claudia asked.

"So you can't talk about me," Evelyn said with a chuckle. She winked at Edith. "She loves bragging about her matchmaking skills."

Claudia laughed. "Well, when you're this good at something."

Edith gasped as she pulled a dress from the rack. "This is what you're good at," she said. "These are amazing." When Declan had been dating a model, she had attended some fashion shows with him—one in New York and one in Paris. But she had never seen anything as beautiful as these dresses.

Her compliment hadn't been meant to distract Claudia, but fortunately it did. She forgot all about matching Edith with a man and instead worked hard to match her with a dress. After a while of trying on different outfits, Edith began to feel like a life-size Barbie doll for the designer.

Finally, Claudia clapped her hands together. "That's it," she proclaimed.

Edith spun around in front of the antique oval mirror and had to agree that the yellow sundress, with the crisscrossed back straps and side slits, was perfect for her.

"I love it," she murmured. She couldn't wait to wear it that evening. She didn't even care that she might be a tad overdressed for a family dinner at a ranch. She wanted to see River's reaction when he saw her dressed up in something other than the jeans or shorts she wore with tank tops around the house.

Thinking of La Bonne Vie brought on a wave of guilt. She needed to return to work. She'd taken a long enough break. So she hurried into the dressing room to slip off the dress and back into her shorts and tank top. With the garment in her hand, she hurried up to the counter and opened her purse to dig out her wallet.

Claudia waved her away. "It's yours. On the house," she said. "A gift."

Edith shook her head. "I appreciate that, but I can't accept it. You're running a business here."

"Sometimes she forgets," Maggie interjected. "And as her accountant, I need to remind her."

"Your business will thrive," Edith predicted. "Your designs are amazing. I knew it from seeing Maggie's wedding gown, but…" Claudia was incredibly talented.

Claudia beamed with pride. "I love designing wedding gowns," she admitted and glanced at Evelyn. "In fact I can't wait to design another…"

"Slow down," Evelyn told her. And she reached for the card Edith held out to swipe through the cash register.

Along with her wallet, Edith had also pulled out a scrap of lace. The pink handkerchief fluttered to the counter as she dropped it.

And Claudia gasped. She stared at it in horror. "Where did you find this?"

Only moments ago the young woman had been joking and laughing. Now she looked so serious and scared that Edith's heartbeat quickened.

"At La Bonne Vie," she replied.

"What is it?" Maggie asked as she stepped closer to the counter.

Claudia reluctantly touched the lace like she was touching a spider, and her hand trembled as she held it up. "It's one of my mother—of Livia's—handkerchiefs."

Edith stared at it, as well. "It's no surprise that I would find it in the house. Some of her stuff is still there."

Her gray eyes narrowed, Claudia examined the piece of lace. "Where exactly did you find it—in her dresser or a chest?"

"No," Edith said as she recalled pulling it out when she'd retrieved her can of pepper spray. "It was under the basement stairs."

Claudia shook her head. "It should be dirty, then. And it's not."

"It's a little dirty," Evelyn said as if trying to assure her.

Claudia sniffed the lace. "But it doesn't smell musty. It doesn't smell like it's been lying on a concrete floor for ten years. In fact, it still smells like her perfume..."

"What are you thinking?" Maggie asked, and her face had paled, as well.

"I'm thinking she's been in the house," Claudia replied. "That she might still be in the house..."

Edith shook her head. "No..." But then she remembered the eyes she'd glimpsed in the darkness that first night. Had they been human?

"The last time one of her handkerchiefs showed up," Claudia said, "it was at a crime scene."

La Bonne Vie was not a crime scene. At least it hadn't been when Edith had left. "River is there alone…"

Claudia was already reaching for her cell.

"Are you calling him?" Edith asked.

She shook her head. "No. He never picks up. I'll call Knox to check on him." But would River's brother get to the estate in time to help him?

Knox found the front door unlocked, so he let himself in. He knew he was trespassing. La Bonne Vie didn't belong to the Coltons anymore. But he doubted *she* would ever accept that. If she had returned to Shadow Creek, this was where she would be. But the house wasn't empty. Edith was staying there. And River was there, as well.

"River?" he called out for his brother. While Edith's car was gone, his brother's truck was parked by the gurgling fountain. He had to be there. Claudia had just called in a panic about their brother being alone at La Bonne Vie. He would have liked to tell her she was overreacting, but now he wasn't so sure. "River?"

Finally he heard something, some weird clanging noise, and the floor nearly vibrated beneath his feet.

Was this the noise that had driven Edith downstairs that night she'd been hurt?

"That's not pipes rattling," he murmured as he headed toward the kitchen. The noise was louder here, and the basement door stood open. He reached for his weapon, but since he was no longer a Ranger, he didn't carry it on him anymore. He had a permit to, though, so maybe he would start again. Now that he knew...

Slowly and quietly, he headed down the stairs—carefully searching the shadows for any signs of movement. The noise came from deeper in the basement, probably from the wine cellar where River had found Edith lying beneath those racks and crates.

His heart pounding fast and hard, he hurried in that direction. As he ducked under the arch of the wine cellar, he noticed the gaping hole in the back wall and gasped. But it wasn't a hole. It was a doorway. And there was another room beyond it. He stepped through that doorway, and as he did, he noticed a flash of movement to his right. He ducked just as the crowbar swung toward his head. "Son of a bitch," he exclaimed, the curse slipping between his lips.

The crowbar dropped onto the concrete floor, and River said, "Oh, my God, I didn't know that was you."

"Well, that's good. I'd hate to think you tried to brain me on purpose," Knox remarked.

"No, no," River assured him, then expelled a ragged sigh. "I didn't know you were here. Why are you here?"

Knox narrowed his eyes and studied his younger brother's face. He looked like he had when they were kids and Knox had caught River playing with his BB gun. Guilty as hell. "I came here to give you a heads-up."

River grinned. "Good. You finally decided to run for sheriff."

Knox sucked in a breath. "We have one."

"We have a joke," River said with a snort of derision. "You would be a sheriff."

"That's not why I'm here," Knox said. Not yet. He had to talk to his wife first.

"Then why?" River asked, and he looked even guiltier, like he'd been caught doing something he shouldn't. And he looked impatient as well, like he wanted Knox to leave so he could get back to it.

"What are you doing?" he asked.

"Uh…" River's face flushed with color. "Edith needs to find everything in the house and inventory it. So I needed to open up these secret rooms."

Knox glanced around the room, but he saw only old wine bottles in this one. Nothing like the other secrets of their mother's that had been discovered and used against her. But the FBI had seized all that evidence already. "She's not in Florida."

River snorted. "I never thought she was. It's too damn hot and humid for her to go there in July."

Knox chuckled. He hadn't thought of that, but his brother was right. "Josh's FBI contacts let him know that they caught the person they'd thought was her. It was just someone she'd hired to pose as her."

"Like in Vegas."

It wasn't a question, but Knox nodded. "So she could be anywhere…" And he glanced around again. If there was one secret room, there was bound to be more. Livia had always gone all out. "I thought I'd better check here." He didn't share that Claudia had called in a panic for Knox to check on him. He didn't want to wound his younger brother's pride.

"She's not here," River said.

"You're a little jumpy, though," Knox pointed out. "You nearly hit me with that crowbar."

River sighed. "I didn't think you were her. Maybe a reporter…"

Knox chuckled.

"You know you're a son of a bitch, too," River told him.

Knox tensed, then realized his brother was referring to the curse he'd uttered when the crowbar had nearly struck him.

"We're both sons of the same bitch," Knox said. A coldhearted one who had no qualms about killing anyone who got in her way.

River sighed. "She needs to be back in prison."

Nobody would be safe until she was.

Chapter 14

The last time River had just walked into La Bonne Vie, Edith had dropped a vase. The times before that, she'd nearly used pepper spray on him. So this time he rang the bell. And thanks to his finding the broken circuit and fixing it, it actually worked now.

After going home to clean up, he was back to pick her up for their date. Had she changed her mind?

The bell rang out from inside the house, echoing throughout the foyer. But nobody opened the door. He heard no footsteps crossing the marble. Through the sidelights he couldn't see any movement, no glimpse of a shadow.

Had he and Knox searched thoroughly enough earlier? That was why Knox had visited—to give him the heads-up and to search to see if Livia could be hiding anywhere inside La Bonne Vie. Had they missed a hiding place?

Edith's vehicle was there, so she should have come to the door already. If she was able…

His heart pounding fast and furiously, he unlocked, pushed open the door and stepped inside the foyer. He was hurrying across it when his heart stopped entirely for a moment—at the sight of Edith coming down the staircase. She'd looked beautiful the night before wearing just an oversize T-shirt. Tonight she was stunning in a yellow dress; she was luminous like a beam of sunshine.

His breath escaped in a shaky sigh. "Wow…"

A smile curved her lips, and at the bottom of the steps, she twirled around. "Isn't it a great dress?" she asked.

He'd barely noticed it. It was the glimpses of skin it exposed and the sleek curves it highlighted that had all of his attention. The straps left her shoulders and most of her back bare, while her toned legs peeked out the side slits. Desire slammed through him, tensing his every muscle. "Yeah," he murmured. "It's great…"

"Claudia designed it. She's so talented."

He couldn't argue with her. "Yeah, she's amazing," he agreed. And he would have to thank her personally for designing this particular dress. It looked like she'd made it specifically for Edith.

"You look beautiful." So damn beautiful that his body ached for her.

Her lips curved into a smile at the compliment. "It's the dress."

It had nothing to do with the dress. He wanted to tell her that, but he wanted to show her even more. He stepped closer to her.

With heels on, she was just a little bit shorter than

him. He wouldn't have to lean down far to brush his mouth across hers. She'd painted her lips, or maybe they only had gloss on them. They were shiny, like her dark hair that she'd curled softly around her face. Now he knew why she hadn't answered the door. She'd been getting ready.

Was all this for him?

"Wow…" he murmured again with a shaky breath.

She lifted a slightly trembling hand to her hair. "I don't know if I should be flattered or insulted," she said. "How bad have I looked the past week?"

"You never looked bad," he assured her. "Not even when I found you on the basement floor."

Her smile slipped away.

And he was sorry he'd brought it up. But it was never far from his mind.

"You really shouldn't be staying here alone," he said. Especially after what Knox had shared with him. But just because Livia wasn't in Florida didn't mean she was here. Why would she keep returning to Shadow Creek?

"I was surprised to find the house empty when I came back from town," she said.

But was it empty? Or was there someone else hiding in it? Someone who would know where all those secret rooms were? River had had a bad feeling about La Bonne Vie even before Knox had confirmed his suspicions that it wasn't their mother who'd been sighted in Florida.

"Claudia told me Knox was coming out to see you," she added. "But neither of you were here when I got back."

"After he left, I went back to Mac's to clean up," he said.

Her gaze moved from his face down his white dress shirt, over his dark jeans to the toes of his black boots. He'd replaced his usual dusty white hat with a clean black one that matched his boots and unfortunately the patch over his eye. But she didn't look repulsed; she looked interested.

And the night before when she'd kissed him...

It had felt like she'd been interested—until she'd pushed him away. Had she done that because she was really worried he might have PTSD? Or had she done it because she'd remembered her boss, who was more than a boss?

But her boss wasn't here tonight. And the closer River could get to her before he arrived, the better. He took another step toward her, but she dodged around him and headed across the foyer, her heels clicking against the marble.

"You didn't have to come back to get me," she said. "This isn't a date."

As if she'd punched him in the gut, he sucked in a breath. He wished it was a date—that she was his girlfriend in addition to being his boss. But how could he have a relationship with anyone when he wasn't even sure who he was anymore? And it wasn't just not knowing his paternity, it was also not knowing who he was without the Corps.

A bodyguard?

Josh's job offer was tempting. Even with one eye, River could do the work. But after fixing up La Bonne Vie, he realized there was a hell of a lot he could do with just one eye.

Like admire the most beautiful woman he'd ever met…

Who was Edith, though? Just an assistant to her boss or more? And was she staying in Shadow Creek, or would she be moving back to wherever she lived when she wasn't working on the house? She'd grown up in New Orleans. Was that where she lived now?

He opened his mouth to ask all those questions. But those were first date type of questions, and she'd made it clear this wasn't a date at all.

"I know," he assured her. "But Mac would kick my ass if I didn't see you there and home." Mac, not the man he'd thought was his father, was who had taught him how to be a gentleman—because Mac was one himself.

So River helped her into his truck and closed the door behind her before going around to the driver's side.

"I didn't think to ask the other day," she said as he slid behind the steering wheel, "when you were driving me to the hospital. But you still have a license?"

He touched the patch and grinned. "Yes. I have twenty-twenty in the left, so I passed the vision tests."

"Are you sure?" she asked. "You ran an awful lot of red lights that day."

He'd been so worried about her. "You wouldn't let me call an ambulance," he reminded her.

"I was fine," she said.

"You have a concussion," he said. And it could have been far worse. "You really shouldn't be staying alone at La Bonne Vie." Especially if she wasn't actually alone in the house.

"I'm fine," she repeated. "I don't want to impose on Uncle Mac."

"Mac wouldn't consider it an imposition at all." But that wasn't what River had meant. Instead of her staying alone in the house, he could stay there, too.

The trip between La Bonne Vie and Mac's ranch was short, and they'd already pulled into the driveway with the other trucks and vehicles. He hesitated before turning off the ignition, though.

He dreaded social events. Even before he'd been injured, he'd hated all the parties his mother had thrown at her estate. He'd hated being put on parade to bolster the image of a loving mother she'd tried to portray. And now that he'd been wounded, he hated social events even more—hated the looks and the pity and the questions.

As if she sensed his discomfort, Edith reached over and covered one of his hands on the steering wheel with one of hers. "They're all family," she said. "It'll be fine."

"You didn't think so when I invited you earlier," he reminded her.

"I didn't think I was invited then," she said. And she'd been hurt.

"I'm sorry," he said.

She squeezed his hand. "Uncle Mac intended to invite me. He just hadn't had the chance yet. Evelyn told me so when I was at Honeysuckle Road."

"Buying that dress…" Even in the dim light, she glimmered like sunshine. He turned off the ignition. But then he hesitated before opening the door. Once they stepped out of the truck, they would no longer be alone. He liked being alone with her—like they'd been the night before, kissing, touching…

He wanted to kiss her now.

And her gaze dipped to his mouth, as if she was tempted to lean closer and brush her lips across his. He drew in a breath and his body tensed in anticipation.

But she shook her head. "We need to get in there," she said. "We're probably late." She didn't reach for her door handle, either. And he doubted it was because she was waiting for him to open it. She'd made it clear earlier that this wasn't a date.

"Nobody was here yet when I left," he said. "So they just got here, too." As if to prove his point, the driver's door of the vehicle in front of them opened. Hawk, Claudia's fiancé, walked around the hood to open the passenger's door for his wife-to-be. The windows of the vehicle were steamed. They'd obviously been doing what River wanted to do with Edith—passionately kiss her.

But before he could close the distance between his mouth and hers, the other couple noticed them and walked toward the truck. He uttered a groan of disappointment. And almost thought he heard an echo of one from Edith.

Had she wanted his kiss?

Had she wanted him the night before as badly as he'd wanted her? He didn't have the chance to ask before Hawk opened her door and the evening began.

For someone who hadn't wanted to attend the dinner party, she seemed very at home—among his family and at the ranch. He didn't know how often she had visited her uncle over the years that they'd reconnected, but it must have been enough times that she knew where everything was inside the house. And she pitched in to help the other women and Mac with dinner.

When River had invited her, she'd claimed they weren't her family except for Mac and Thorne, but yet she fit in with the Coltons better than he ever had. Like Claudia, he needed to find out who he really was. Maybe then he would feel like he belonged here, too. Right now he longed to be back at La Bonne Vie. He needed to search for more of those secret rooms and the secrets they hopefully held.

"Are you sure you're all right?" Uncle Mac asked her as he stared at her forehead.

Edith had curled her hair to cover the small wound. Nobody else had commented on it, but Mac had seen it in the hospital. So he knew where it was.

"Yes, I'm fine," she said with a reassuring smile. She was having a great time at the party. "Evelyn is wonderful."

"See," Claudia said as she joined them in the kitchen. "I do a great job matchmaking."

Mac slid his arm around her. "You won't get an argument from me," he said with a big grin.

Edith's heart warmed with her uncle's happiness.

"Who's she trying to set you up with?" Mac asked. Then he followed Claudia's gaze to where River stood in the living room, near the front door, as if he was tempted to sneak out. And he shook his head. "Not River…"

Edith's heart lurched now. Why didn't her uncle want her involved with one of the kids he'd helped raise?

"Why not?" Claudia asked.

Mac shook his head again. "He's not ready," he told her. "He's been through so much. He still seems so lost."

Claudia uttered a pitying sigh. "I know. I understand—probably better than anyone."

If even half the media reports had been accurate, the beautiful designer had been through a lot. She'd only recently learned her biological mother had been one of Livia's sex trafficking victims. And another of those victims had tried to kill her. But thanks to the PI who was now her fiancé, she hadn't been harmed. So how could she compare what she'd endured to what River and probably some of his fellow Marines had gone through?

"It's not just *that*," Mac said.

And Edith was wondering what *that* was. Especially when Mac continued, "He's still battling the nightmares over whatever happened on that last deployment."

"It was horrible, no doubt," Claudia agreed and a shimmer of tears came to her eyes. She looked from her brother back to Edith. "That's why he needs something beautiful in his life, to replace the ugliness."

But Mac shook his head.

And Edith didn't know whom her uncle was trying to protect from Claudia's matchmaking. Her or River.

"It doesn't matter whether or not he's ready," Edith interrupted them. "I'm not interested." Which was a lie. She was very much interested in River. Her skin still tingled from how he'd looked at her when he'd first seen her in the dress, like he wanted to take it off her.

And she'd wanted him to do just that. She'd wanted him to kiss her and touch her—so badly that she'd nearly kissed him in his truck—when he'd looked so hesitant about joining his own family. Now she understood why. Their concern was nearly too much.

It wasn't just what Claudia and Mac were saying, either. It was the way the others watched him—like he was about to fall apart. Did none of them realize how strong he was?

He had survived a horrible injury, a horrible loss, and he didn't feel sorry for himself. He forged ahead as if nothing was wrong with him.

"Why?" Claudia asked, her curvy body tensing. She didn't look happy or sad now. She looked fierce and defensive—of her brother. "Is it the eye? The scars?"

"No."

"That might be a problem for some women," Claudia continued. "But I thought you—"

"Claudia," Mac cautioned her. His loyalty probably felt divided between them—his niece and the girl he'd raised like a daughter.

"I am not interested in anyone right now," Edith clarified. "I am much too busy at La Bonne Vie."

"Doing what?" Thorne asked the question.

Edith hadn't even noticed her cousin step into the kitchen. She stared at him in silence.

"I can ask River," he said. "He's been working up there with you."

"And he won't answer your question, either," River answered for himself.

"Did she make you sign a confidentiality agreement, too?" Thorne asked.

River snorted. "No. I'm just not an idiot."

Maggie rubbed her hand down her husband's tense arm. "I'm sure we'll all know soon enough," she said.

"Or whoever her boss is might intend to let it sit empty for another ten years," Thorne replied.

Edith doubted that. Declan hadn't built SinCo into the billion-dollar operation it was by making bad investments. But she was curious, too, about his intentions for the estate. When he visited, she was going to find out.

"It's not empty now," she said. "I'm staying there. And I need to get back." She sent an imploring glance to River.

"You shouldn't be staying there alone," Mac said.

What was he implying? That she should invite River to stay with her? Her pulse quickened at the thought, at the temptation. But then her uncle added, "You should be staying here."

Of course he wouldn't suggest she and River stay together. He didn't think one of them was good enough for the other.

"Yes," Thorne agreed with his father. "It's too dangerous to stay there alone."

Edith touched the wound on her forehead. "That was an accident."

"Maggie told me about the handkerchief you found there," Thorne said.

"Handkerchief?" Mac asked.

"It was one of Moth—of Livia's," Claudia answered for her. "She said she found it under the basement stairs but it wasn't that dirty, didn't smell musty…" Her voice cracked as she trailed off.

"Where is it?" River asked, and he looked at Edith.

"I kept it," Claudia replied. "I'm going to have Leonor give it to Josh."

"Or give it to Knox," River said. He drew in a deep

breath before sharing, "He told me earlier that she's not in Florida."

Claudia shivered, and Mac tightened his arm around her. "That doesn't mean she's here."

Hawk drew his fiancée away from Mac and into his own arms. "And if she is, she isn't going to hurt you."

Mac shook his head. "She's not here. She's too smart to risk coming back to Shadow Creek again."

She wasn't there, but talk of Livia had effectively ended the Colton family dinner party.

Livia loved a party. And she was half tempted to show up at the one at Mac's. Wouldn't they all be surprised to see her? Or would they?

She'd overheard Knox and River earlier. The authorities knew she was not in Florida. Apparently River had suspected all along.

Was she the reason River kept searching the secret rooms in the basement? Was he looking for her?

She could understand the others wanting to find her. Knox was a lawman. So was Leonor's new fiancé, the FBI man who'd been using her to find Livia. When would the girl learn to not trust men? She sighed and focused again on her youngest son.

River had never showed much interest in her or in La Bonne Vie when he'd been living there. He showed interest in Edith Beaulieu, though.

From the panic room with its security monitors and intercoms, Livia hadn't missed much that took place in the house. She'd nearly panicked earlier when River had found the doorway in the room off the wine cellar. But he hadn't found the one to the panic room.

Maybe he thought only one room opened off each other secret room. That was good. For him.

Because if he came back and found the entrance to this room, she would have to pull the trigger she'd cocked earlier. He wasn't a lawman like Knox or Josh, but River had always had a sense of honor and obligation. Or he wouldn't have become a Marine and spent ten years in the Corps.

Or had he only done that to get away from the scandal? From the attention that came with being a Colton? He'd always hated that—just like he'd always hated parties.

She had no doubt that he would be back soon—to the house—to search for her secrets. If he found them, he would die. It didn't matter that he was her son. She wasn't going back to prison.

She had too much left to do…

Chapter 15

"Thank you for bringing me home," Edith murmured over her shoulder as she unlocked the front door of La Bonne Vie. While gracious, she also sounded dismissive, like she was trying to get rid of him.

She was probably worried that he was going to try something again. And he totally intended to.

When she opened the door, he stepped inside with her and shut it behind them. She turned toward him, her dark eyes wide with surprise. "What are you doing?"

"The other night you told me I could do whatever I wanted," he reminded her.

And she took a step back. "I—I was talking about work. Not…"

"This?" he asked. And he closed the distance between them and took the kiss he'd been wanting the entire evening. His lips moved over the silkiness of hers.

Then he deepened the kiss. Before the passion burning inside him could overwhelm and consume him, he pulled back and expelled an unsteady breath. Damn. It was hot. So hot he wanted to take off his shirt and the rest of his clothes…

She was so damn hot. He wanted to take off her clothes.

But she stared up at him with an expression he couldn't read. Was it fear?

After all the talk earlier, he didn't blame her. "I shouldn't have brought you here," he said. "It isn't home."

Her brow furrowed slightly as if she was confused and couldn't follow his train of thought. "I—I know it's not my home. It was yours—"

He snorted. "I don't think it was ever my home, either." He glanced at the ornate staircase behind her. "It was my mother's stage."

She glanced behind her at the stairwell, then wrapped her arms around herself and shivered. "Do *you* think she would come back here?"

"I don't know…" He hadn't thought so, but then Livia was unpredictable. "When did you find that handkerchief?"

"The day after you heard me scream," she said. "I found it when I retrieved my can of pepper spray from under the basement stairs."

"Claudia doesn't think it's been there ten years," he said. And dread gripped his stomach, tightening the muscles. Could Livia have been in the house? Was she now?

He walked toward the kitchen, toward the basement stairs where Edith had found the scrap of lace.

"We don't know she dropped it," Edith said as she followed him. "The FBI searched the house again after her escape, right? They could have moved something and dropped it then."

That was true. And made him feel a little better. But he knew what would make him feel even better. Her.

Even though she hadn't shoved him away after the kiss, she hadn't pulled him back in for another, either. She apparently wasn't as affected as he'd been.

"I'm going to look around again," he said. "Make sure nobody is down there."

She didn't stop him from heading down the stairs, nor did she follow him. Maybe all the talk of Livia had unnerved her, as well.

But she'd still insisted on coming back to La Bonne Vie instead of staying at Mac's. He didn't understand why she was so stubborn. Neither had the others. She'd insisted she had too much work to do—as if the short commute would prevent her from inventorying more than an item or two.

Hell. He needed to tell her about the new room he'd discovered—about all the wine. Maybe that find would make her happy enough to forgive his snooping around for secrets. Maybe it would make her boss happy enough to let a Colton keep working for him.

Ultimately River worked for whomever Edith did. Who the hell was that?

Everyone else had wanted to know, as well. That was why River had driven her away from the ranch. He knew how it was to be bombarded with questions you didn't want to or couldn't answer.

He and Knox had thoroughly searched the basement earlier. So River's search was more perfunctory now. He just did a quick sweep looking for intruders. But when he stepped into the room he'd discovered earlier, he lingered.

He'd found one secret door off it. But what if there was another? He'd heard something earlier that day— something that had sounded like the telltale click of a gun cocking. Maybe it had just been his imagination.

But he had that eerie feeling again that raised the short hairs on the nape of his neck, like he was not alone. This wasn't just his imagination, either—because he could hear someone else breathing. He could almost feel them breathing...

He whirled around to find a woman standing behind him.

"What the hell is this?" Edith asked as she glanced around the room off the wine cellar. With its racks and crates, it just appeared to be another wine cellar.

River's broad shoulders lifted in a shrug. "I found it earlier today. It's one of my mother's secret stashes." Instead of sounding triumphant over the discovery, he sounded disappointed.

Edith felt a little disappointed herself as she surveyed all the dust-covered bottles. She reached out for one, but River caught her wrist and pulled her hand away. Maybe he didn't want the racks toppling over onto them both, like they had the last time she'd picked a bottle off a shelf.

"You'll get your dress dirty," he explained with an appreciative glance at her.

She glanced down at the dress she loved. "You're right. I don't want to ruin it."

"Then you shouldn't even be down here," he told her. "Why are you?"

She held up the can of pepper spray she'd retrieved from her purse. She'd been worried about him and hadn't wanted him confronting danger alone and unarmed.

"That probably wouldn't even faze my mother," he remarked, and again there was a trace of disappointment in his voice.

"Is she invincible?" Edith asked.

He sighed. "Seems that way."

"That must be where you get it," she said.

He chuckled and touched the scar on the side of his handsome face. "This tells another story."

"You're alive," she said.

He sighed again—this time heavily. "Yeah, not everyone else was as lucky…"

Her heart lurched as she realized how close he must have come to dying. And selfishly she thought of how she might never have met him.

That emptiness inside her stretched wider. But how could he create a hole he'd never filled?

"I'm sorry," she said.

He shook his head. "Wasn't your fault."

But she had a feeling he had assigned blame to someone. Himself. She had no idea how to ease his guilt over not being able to save someone when she had never been able to ease her own.

"You choose a bottle," she said. "And meet me upstairs."

She left him alone then, knowing that might be what he needed to deal with the demons she'd brought up. Everyone else pushed and hovered over him, and that made him shut down, like she'd seen him do at Mac's ranch. When it was just the two of them, he was more relaxed, more what she suspected was his true self.

She felt that way around him as well, like she was her true self. Like he wouldn't judge her for her failures or for her fears...

So why hadn't she told him everything the other night? Why had she let him believe she was worried about his sanity, when she was really worried about her own?

Probably because she knew she wasn't like Livia Colton. She was not invincible. The kiss he'd given her earlier had proved that; it had shaken her to her core, made her ache and pulse for him.

Her pulse quickened just thinking about his mouth on hers. He hadn't even touched her.

She'd only missed two days of running but she felt winded when she reached the top of the stairwell. She walked over and leaned against the kitchen cabinets to catch her breath. River made her heart race more than any run ever had.

"Are you okay?" River asked when he joined her seconds later.

Edith pressed a hand against her heart.

"Did you see something down there?" he asked anxiously with a glance back toward the stairs.

She'd seen him. Clearly. And she was afraid she was beginning to fall for him.

She shook her head, denying her thought and his fear. "No. I didn't see anything." She lifted the hem of her dress. "Stairs and heels aren't a good combination."

He looked skeptical—probably because he'd watched her descend them earlier without the slightest bit of trouble. Then he turned his attention to the bottle of wine. He washed it off in the sink and wiped it down with a towel. "I have no idea what constitutes a good bottle of wine."

"For me," she said, "it's not too dry or too sweet."

He stared at her for a long moment. "Are you talking about the wine?"

"Of course…"

He stepped closer, trapping her between his body and the counter. Then he lowered his head until his lips nearly touched hers and murmured, "I thought you were talking about my kiss…"

Her heart slammed against her ribs. She could taste him on her lips. But yet only his breath touched her mouth. He didn't close the distance between them. He didn't kiss her again.

And she wanted him to—desperately. But it was that desperation that scared her so much. She tilted her head back, away from his and said, "Maybe the wine was a bad idea. It's already quite late."

He narrowed his eye and studied her face. "I've done it again."

"What?"

"That's what I'd like to know," he said. "It's whatever I did the other night that makes you change your mind about us."

"There is no 'us,'" she said. "There is you and me—separately—and only working together."

"Then what is *this*?" he asked, and he ran his fingertip along her throat where her pulse pounded so quickly that he must have been able to see it. "What's this attraction between us?"

"Bad judgment," she replied.

"You feel it, too."

She felt more than she ever had before—more than she ever wanted to feel. She shook her head, denying her feelings to him and herself. "No."

"Liar." He called her on it.

"It's a bad idea for us to do anything other than work together," she said.

"Why?" he asked. "Because I'm too damaged for you?" He touched his scar.

And Edith cursed him. "That's not it and you know it."

"The other night you were worried about my PTSD," he said.

"I shouldn't have said that."

"Why?" he asked.

"Because I don't know anything about what you went through and how you've handled it."

"My sister Leonor's fiancé knows," he said. "And he offered me a job in his new security firm, so he must not be too concerned."

"He's not dating you," she said, and before he could say anything more, she added, "And neither am I."

"Why not?" River asked. "If it isn't because you're worried I'm going to crack, what is it?"

"It's complicated," she said.

"Is it your boss?" he asked.

Declan would feel betrayed that she had hired a Colton. If she dated one, she shuddered to think how he'd feel. And she didn't want to hurt him.

"That's part of it," she admitted.

"Who is this guy to you?" River asked. "I know he's more than your boss."

Was that jealousy she detected in his deep voice? In

his tightly clenched jaw? He leaned closer and brushed his mouth across hers, nibbling at her lips. She was helpless to do anything but moan.

He pulled back and remarked, "But yet he's not important enough that you didn't kiss me back."

"I…" Had. She'd kissed him. And she wanted to kiss him again. So badly. "I can't do this."

He backed off and held up his hands, but they trembled slightly. "I know. I know. It's complicated."

"For you, too," she pointed out.

"You're right," he agreed. "So I'll stay here. But I'll stay out of your bed."

"We both know if you stay here that won't happen," she said. Because she would be the one inviting him to join her, to fill that emptiness aching inside her. "You checked the house," she reminded him. "Nobody's here but us."

And "us" was a bad idea. They both knew it. He must have agreed because he didn't argue. He just nodded and headed toward the front door. She heard him lock and close it behind himself.

Then she felt her knees begin to shake. But that was a good thing. If they weren't, she might have chased after him and begged him to come back. And when, moments later, she heard a clanking noise coming from the basement, she wished she had.

"It's nothing," she murmured to herself. River had searched the basement. He'd found that secret room full of wine but nothing and nobody else. It had to be pipes rattling.

She tightened her grasp on her canister of pepper spray. But she wasn't about to go investigate again. She might not have learned anything from all those hor-

ror movies, but she'd learned a lot from the night she'd
spent lying on the concrete. So she closed the basement
door and propped the back of one of the kitchen chairs
under the knob. Hopefully it would not turn. Whatever
was down there would damn well stay down there until
Edith was ready to deal with it.

And she wasn't ready tonight.

Just in case that chair didn't keep the knob from
turning, she hurried upstairs to the master bedroom.
Those doors had a lock, which she turned after clos-
ing them. She was safe in there.

But she could still hear things in the house, the
clanking noise echoing throughout it. She hurriedly
changed from her dress to yoga pants and a sweatshirt,
but she was still chilled.

And scared…

She could have called someone. Uncle Mac. Thorne.
Then she'd have to hear them say they'd told her so.
They'd told her not to stay there alone.

However, it didn't necessarily sound like she was
alone right now. Was there someone else inside La
Bonne Vie?

Thorne waited in the dark. He had hoped he was
waiting for nothing. But then he heard the truck and
saw the headlights coming down the driveway. He
leaned back against the ranch house so the high beams
wouldn't blind him.

Then he flinched, thinking of how his brother was
blinded now. In one eye.

But it didn't affect his vision that much. River must
have glimpsed him in the shadows. Because the minute

he shut off the truck and stepped out of it, he headed toward Mac's front porch. "Hey, Thorne."

"You came back," Thorne said. And even though he'd been waiting for him, he was disappointed to see him.

"You did, too," River said.

Thorne had left when River had with Edith. He'd taken his pregnant wife home where she could rest. She was exhausted. But he was too restless to stay with her. He would have only kept her awake. He paced his father's front porch instead, while he'd been waiting for River. "I hoped you were going to stay up there to protect her."

But yet, knowing his fiercely independent cousin, he had also been pretty certain that Edith wouldn't let River stay.

"You think that would have been a good thing?" he asked his brother with an arched brow.

River was apparently not going to get over what he'd overheard Thorne and Mac saying about him the other night, about how he could be damaged from whatever had happened to him. Thorne could have kicked himself for being an insensitive ass.

"I think it's better for you to be there," Thorne said, "than for her to be alone if our mother is hiding out in that house."

"I checked it out," River said. "I couldn't find any evidence of her being there."

"The handkerchief—"

"Proves nothing," River said.

But Thorne wondered if his brother was trying to convince him of that or himself.

"She could have dropped that anytime," River said.

Thorne nodded. "I hope she dropped it ten years ago, but that's not what Claudia thinks. And she knows all about fabrics and perfume and stuff." And according to Maggie, she'd been scared when that handkerchief had fallen out of Edith's purse.

"She could have gone into the house when she was in town before," River said.

River hadn't been back in town yet when their mother had killed the man who'd kidnapped her only grandchild. He must have been on that last mission— the one that had nearly killed him. But of course River had heard about what their mother had done—if not from family, then from the media. Livia was infamous for exacting her own form of justice while eluding it for the crimes she'd committed.

Thorne expelled a shaky sigh. "That's true. She might not be anywhere near Shadow Creek."

"Let's hope that's the case," River said.

"What about Edith?" Thorne asked.

"What about her?" River said, and he sounded unnerved now.

Did he think Thorne was asking about his intentions toward his cousin? He suppressed a grin of amusement. There was nothing funny about the current situation.

"Do you really think she's safe up there by herself?" Thorne clarified his question.

River shrugged and murmured a heartfelt, "I hope so…"

But he didn't know so.

But then, with Livia on the loose, how could anyone know what would happen?

Chapter 16

The sun wasn't even up when River headed out to his truck. Hell, he should have just slept in it last night— in the driveway of La Bonne Vie. The gurgling fountain might have lulled him to sleep. Then he would have actually gotten some. He'd lain awake the entire night, worrying about Edith being alone in the house.

But had she really been alone?

Despite him and Knox searching it, nobody knew how many secret rooms Livia had had built in the basement.

For some reason all of the tradesmen and architects who'd worked on the house for Livia had died under mysterious circumstances. No one was safe from the woman. Not even her own kids.

And certainly not Edith.

He'd pressed so hard on the accelerator that he arrived at the gates within minutes of leaving the ranch. He touched the remote clipped to his visor. But the gates barely opened before he drove through them and up to the house. Since it was so early, he didn't ring the bell. He just let himself inside and peered around the shadows in the foyer.

Was it just the trees outside blocking out that first light of dawn? Or was someone inside?

"Edith?" he called out for her. But there was no flurry of movement. If she was up, she would have been working on something. Edith Beaulieu was probably physically incapable of doing nothing. He headed up the stairwell and took the hallway that led down to the double doors of the master suite.

The doors were closed.

She must have been asleep yet. He could have gone back downstairs and started working. But instead he headed toward those doors, taking slow, measured steps to muffle the noise of his boots against the worn Oriental runner. He needed to check on her, make sure she was all right.

He'd spent the entire night worrying about her being alone in this house. Even after he'd checked it out, he wasn't certain there wasn't someplace someone could hide in La Bonne Vie. In fact, he was pretty certain there were a lot of places someone could hide, especially someone who'd had those secret spots built.

He stopped outside the doors and listened. But he could hear nothing from within the room. He reached for the knob and tried to turn it, but the doors were locked.

"Who's there?" a shaky voice asked. Then it rose

and became stronger, "I have pepper spray. Don't try
to come in here!"

"I know you have pepper spray," River assured her.
"It's me."

He heard running footsteps from within the mas-
sive suite, then the lock clicked and the doors opened.
She threw her arms around his neck and clutched his
shoulders. Her body trembled against his.

"Edith," he said, his heart slamming against his ribs.
He loved her reaction to seeing him, but he doubted it
had anything to do with desire.

She seemed scared to death.

He eased her back and looked at her face, her eyes
were wide and wild with fear. "Oh, my God," he murmured. "What happened? Are you all right?"

She shook her head. "No, someone was in here."

"In here?" he asked, glancing around the room.

"No, no," she said. "I came up here and locked the
doors. But right after you left, I heard something in
the basement again."

"But instead of checking it out, you came up here."
He expelled a shaky breath of relief. "That's good. But
you should have called me."

"You had just looked around the basement. You said
nobody was down there."

"Nobody was when I looked," he said.

She shivered. "So maybe it was the just pipes or
some animals…"

He hadn't seen any animals, either. "You still should
have called someone."

She shook her head. "I didn't want to seem like I was
overreacting…" Tears glistened in her eyes.

And he understood. She didn't want anyone thinking she was like her mother, hearing and seeing things that weren't there.

He pulled her close and held her, rubbing his hand over her back to soothe her fears. "You're not just hearing things. We both know this house has made some weird sounds."

She leaned back and looked up at him hopefully. "That's right. You heard them, too—that day I found you downstairs with the crowbar. Right?"

That was the excuse he'd given her that day. But it wasn't the truth. He had heard an odd noise downstairs, though—that click that had sounded like a gun cocking. But he didn't want to mention that and scare her even more.

So he just nodded and replied, "That's how I found that room off the wine cellar."

She expelled a shaky breath of relief. "That's good. I wasn't sure…"

If she'd really heard the noises or if she'd only imagined them…

"I wish you would have called me," he said. He hated to think of how she'd spent the night, locked in the bedroom, awake and afraid.

"I'll look around again now." But when he moved to step back, she clutched him, her arms winding tightly around his shoulders as her body pressed against his.

His heart lurched in his chest. He'd never felt this way before—so protective and possessive and involved. And now he was scared.

He didn't even know who he was or what he was going to do once his job at La Bonne Vie was over. He had no business falling for someone when he had nothing to offer that person. He pulled back and assured her, "You'll be okay. You have your pepper spray."

Her lips curved into a slight smile, and she nodded. "Thank you," she said, and she rose up on tiptoe and pressed a kiss to his cheek—right over the scar running down it.

A sensation spread from his heart throughout his body, warming him. But still he was chilled. He wasn't afraid of what he might find downstairs. He was afraid of what he'd found here—with Edith.

Edith stared at the closed doors for several moments before she moved. But she didn't do as River had told her. She didn't lock herself back inside the master suite. She'd spent enough time cowering in the dark.

She was not a coward. She'd proved that to the older kids in the foster home when she'd watched those horror movies with them. Now she needed to prove it to herself. Not wanting to go downstairs barefoot, she shoved her feet into a pair of tennis shoes and tied up the laces. In case she needed to run...

She had the can of pepper spray for protection, though. River had nothing but his bare hands. He was strong. She'd witnessed his strength with all the work he'd done around the estate. So she shouldn't be worried about him—especially if the noises were the nothing she had spent the entire night trying to convince herself they were.

But what if they weren't nothing? What if someone else was inside the house? They shouldn't be there. So what might they do to remain undetected?

Hurt River?

He had already been hurt so badly—the scar, the eye.

He'd lost so much. She had to make sure she hadn't sent him off to another battle he might lose. She hurried down the hall toward the stairwell. The sun was coming up, shining through the windows and glinting off the marble floor of the foyer.

The house wasn't scary now. But even with the sun shining in it, it felt cold and impersonal. She couldn't imagine growing up here. Before her father's death, her family had lived in a cute little house that had overflowed with warmth and laughter. But when he'd died, so had the laughter.

Ignoring the pang in her heart, she shrugged off the memories. She certainly hadn't been through as much as River had. She had no right to self-pity.

The rubber soles of her shoes slapped against the marble as she hurried through the foyer to the hall leading back to the kitchen and that basement stairwell. The door stood open at the top.

She could hear no noises now. In fact, the house had been almost eerily silent for a while. But even though it had been quiet, it hadn't felt empty.

She still hadn't felt as though she were alone. And she wasn't really alone. But as she descended the stairs, she caught no glimpse of River in the shadows.

He was probably down the hall by the wine cellar where he'd found that secret room of vintages.

If she hadn't been wearing that lovely dress Claudia had designed, Edith would have checked out the room more. She had the chance now. But as she stepped through the wine cellar and into that room, she found nothing but wine.

There was no sign of River.

Now her heart began to beat fast with fear. "River?" she called out for him.

He had gone downstairs. He would have had to—or else that chair would have still been under the door handle. Unless someone else had knocked that chair aside and left the door open...

Was that the cause of some of the noises she'd heard the night before? The sounds had been so weird and had seemed to echo throughout the central air system, like someone had been pounding on something near the furnace.

Maybe she needed to look in the utility room. But she was so certain he'd be here that she took another look around it. And her heart jumped with fear as she noticed his hat lying in a corner of the room. Something stained the white material. Probably dirt from the concrete floor. But as she picked it up, the dirt smeared across her fingers. It was warm and sticky and red.

It wasn't dirt at all. It was blood.

There was blood on his hat. He had been hurt. He was bleeding. But where the hell was he?

River lay lifeless on the concrete floor. Blood oozed from the wound on his forehead and trailed along the ridge of the scar on his cheek. He had survived whatever had left that scar and taken his eye.

But would he survive the blow he'd just received?

Livia dropped the crowbar onto the floor beside him. And he shifted and moaned at the noise.

And beyond the stone wall, a gasp was audible. The woman was out there. She'd been frantically calling his name, concern and fear apparent in her voice.

How far would she go to find him? Would she find

the same secret room that River just had? He'd found the latch so quickly that Livia had barely had time to arm herself before he stepped through the doorway.

Had he seen her?

Maybe it would be better to end it now—for him and the Beaulieu woman—than to risk either of them finding her. But what would happen when they disappeared?

How long would it be before someone missed them?

Probably not long enough for Livia to accomplish what she'd returned to Shadow Creek to do.

"Damn it," she murmured.

Why did River always have to play the hero? It had obviously nearly gotten him killed when he'd been a Marine. And now...

And now, doing the same for Edith Beaulieu had nearly gotten him killed, as well. If he regained consciousness and saw her, he would die.

Even though he was her son, Livia would have no choice. She would have to take away the life she'd given him twenty-eight years ago.

Chapter 17

Panic pressed on River's lungs when he opened his left eye but couldn't see anything. Had he lost his vision in that eye, as well? Pain reverberated inside his skull, threatening to shatter it. He flinched and blinked and finally his vision cleared.

But the room was dark. He could see only shadows. Was he alone? Where the hell was he?

The last thing he remembered was opening that secret door in the secret room off the wine cellar. But as he'd stepped through it, something had struck him. Hard.

And everything had gone black.

Rolling to his side, he reached out to press his palm against the concrete to lever himself up. But his hand hit something cold and metallic. The crowbar rattled against the floor. And he realized what had struck him.

But who had been wielding it? He'd seen nothing. Not even the crowbar coming at him.

He peered around the room. What was stashed in here? No person. He could discern no shadows in the corners of the small space. So who'd hit him? And where had he or she gone?

To get Edith?

He pushed himself up and regained his feet. But his legs wobbled, threatening to fold beneath him. And he was light-headed, black spots dancing before his still slightly blurred vision.

He reached up to the bump on his forehead. Blood oozed from it, smearing his fingertips and trailing down his face. He straightened the patch that had slipped off his wounded eye socket. Edith didn't need to see that.

Edith. Where was she?

Had the person who'd struck him gone after her now?

Hopefully she was still locked in the master suite, armed with her canister of pepper spray. She would use it—if she had to.

She would be safe. Wouldn't she?

Unless she'd come down here, looking for him, and been blindsided, as well.

He spared the room another longing glance. He wanted to search it. But he could see no journals or papers in plain sight. He would have to look for hiding places or secret safes within the room. And he didn't have time. He had to make sure that Edith was safe.

If it had been his mother who'd struck him, Livia would have no qualms about killing Edith. She appar-

ently had had none about killing him because she'd
struck him nearly hard enough to do the job.

No. If Livia was in the house, then Edith wasn't
safe no matter where she was. Livia would have keys
to the master suite. Hell, she probably had a secret passageway to it. Maybe that was why Edith had heard so
many noises the night before.

Livia had been walking her secret passageways.

But why?

Why would she come back to La Bonne Vie?

What the hell did she want?

The same thing River did—her secrets?

But while River wanted to learn the truth, Livia
would do anything to keep it hidden. Even kill.

Edith clutched her cell phone in one hand and her
canister of pepper spray in the other as she headed
back down the stairwell from the second floor. The
Shadow Creek dispatcher was on the line, assuring her
that the sheriff was personally on his way to respond
to her call for help.

She should have called them last night, instead of
lying awake and in fear of what might be in the house
with her. Now she knew something was—and that
something had hurt River. She blinked several times,
fighting back the tears that threatened to fill her eyes.

Where was he?

River. Not the sheriff—although she needed him,
too. She needed him to help her find River.

"I think you should send an ambulance, too," she
told the woman, remembering how she'd found the hat
with his blood smeared on it.

"You said you weren't hurt," the dispatcher reminded her. Like a kindly grandmother, that had been her first question. *Are you hurt, honey?* Then, *Do you need an ambulance?*

And Edith had replied with No and No. She was fine. She didn't need an ambulance. She wasn't certain what River needed, though.

"But my…"

What?

What was River to her?

Employee? Friend? Not her lover. She kept sending him away, and maybe that was another mistake, like the one she had made when she'd let River go alone into the basement to investigate. She should have been there with him. Then she'd know where the hell he was and how badly he was hurt.

"Friend," she concluded. "My friend went to check out the noises I heard, and now I can't find him. He must be hurt."

"You said someone's in the house and someone else is missing," the dispatcher recited as if she was reading back notes she'd taken during the call. "Who is missing? What is your friend's name?"

Just as she'd struggled to label what he was to her, she struggled to reveal his name. She knew he valued his privacy. But this was the sheriff's office. Surely, they wouldn't say anything to the reporters swarming around town.

"River Colton," she replied.

"River Colton?" the woman repeated, and her voice had dropped to a salacious whisper, like she was gossiping in church and didn't want the preacher catching her. "He's your friend?" she asked. "He hasn't been back in Shadow Creek very long."

Those didn't seem like questions the dispatcher needed to ask to assess the situation at the estate.

"My uncle is Mac Mackenzie," Edith said.

"Oh," the woman replied as if that answered all of her questions. But then she started in with more. "What are you doing at La Bonne Vie?"

What were the privacy laws regarding 9-1-1 calls? So many were released every day because of the Freedom of Information Act. Maybe calling the Shadow Creek Sheriff's Department hadn't been a good idea.

She should have called Uncle Mac instead. Or Thorne. But she hadn't wanted them getting hurt— like River.

A scraping noise emanated from the basement. And Edith trembled in fear. "Where's the sheriff?" she asked.

It seemed like she'd been on the phone an awfully long time.

"He was down at the Cozy Diner when you called, honey," the woman said. "But I'm sure he's on his way to La Bonne Vie right now."

Edith doubted he would get there in time. Someone was definitely moving around downstairs again. "I—I have to go," she told the woman.

"But you're supposed to stay on the line until—"

Edith disconnected. She needed to call someone she knew would actually help her. But when she pressed the contact for Uncle Mac, the call went immediately to his voice mail. Her fingers trembling, she pressed Thorne's next but got his voice mail, as well.

What about Maggie? Did she have her number? She didn't have time to scroll through her phone and find out, though. The noises below had grown louder.

She probably should have run outside—to her car. But she could think only of River. If there was some way to help him, then she had to try. So she shoved her phone into her pocket and started down the steps with both hands on her canister of pepper spray so she wouldn't drop it this time. So she would be able to use it if she needed to…

Something moved in the shadows, lurching forward, then stumbling over to lean against the wall. A groan emanated from the shadows.

A groan she recognized.

"River!" Her feet barely touched the last few steps as she ran to him. "Are you okay?"

He levered himself away from the wall. "Yeah, yeah…" But he seemed distracted, groggy. Then he focused on her, studying her face. "You're okay? You're not hurt?"

"No." Her heart warmed that he had been concerned about her—even as he was obviously in pain himself. She reached out and gently touched the bump on his head. The blood was beginning to dry, so only a few drops smeared her fingertips. "This looks bad." Worse than the wound she'd gotten from the wine bottle. "You must have a concussion."

"I've got a hell of a headache," he murmured.

She was right. The dispatcher should have sent an ambulance. Edith wouldn't be able to carry River up the stairs like he had so effortlessly carried her.

"Help's coming," she assured him—and herself.

He shook his head now. "I don't need it. I'm fine."

She skimmed her fingertips from his wound down the side of his face. Blood had dried along his scar. "You're not fine. You're hurt. What happened?"

His broad shoulders lifted in a shrug. "I don't know…"

"Where were you?" she asked. "I was just down here and I couldn't find you. But I found your hat with blood on it. I looked everywhere for you."

"I—"

Before he could reply, the doorbell rang. Then someone pounded on the door.

"Who's that?" River asked as his body tensed. He was immediately alert, stepping between her and the stairs leading down from the kitchen.

"It's probably the—"

"Sheriff Jeffries," a voice called out from above. "You reported a break-in."

And if they'd been the intruders, they would have had a chance to escape him.

River groaned again.

"Are you okay?" she asked as she slid under his arm.

"You shouldn't have called *him*," River admonished her.

"Why not?" she asked. Had he been doing something down there or discovered something down there that he didn't want the sheriff to see?

"Because he feels the same way about the Coltons that your boss does," River replied. "He hates us."

She saw that the moment the sheriff descended the stairs and joined them in the basement.

"I thought you were missing, River," Sheriff Jeffries remarked as if he was disappointed he wasn't. With his thinning blond hair, the man looked older than River, so she doubted they had any kind of personal rivalry going back to when River had lived in Shadow Creek before joining the Marines.

Was his animosity only because River's last name was Colton? Anger coursed through her at the injustice of that prejudice. But then she remembered that it was one Declan shared—one she had shared before she'd grown up and realized she had no reason to resent them. It wasn't their fault she had wound up in foster care.

"He's been hurt," she said. "You need to call for an ambulance."

The sheriff stepped closer to River, but he was shorter and had to peer up at his wound. "Doesn't look that serious. You hit your head on something?"

River touched his fingers to the bump and replied, "I don't know what happened."

And Edith believed him—while the sheriff narrowed his dark eyes as if skeptical.

"How the hell could you miss it?" he asked. "Looks like you walked right into it." Then his thin lips curved into a slight, almost mocking grin. "Oh, that's right. You're half-blind now."

Edith gasped at his remark. It went beyond insensitive to almost cruel. "Sheriff," she said, bristling with anger. "I called you here to help—"

River chuckled now. "Told you that was a mistake," he murmured.

She completely understood and agreed now.

"Why did you call?" the sheriff asked. "You were hearing *noises*?" He sounded as if he was mocking her now.

Did he know about her mother? About the things she'd heard that weren't there?

River slid his arm around her shoulders. He was either offering his support or using her for support as he leaned against her slightly.

The sheriff's already beady eyes narrowed as he took in the familiarity between her and River. "Miss Emmie said you two are *friends*?"

Edith's anger grew at his obvious insinuation that they were more than friends. But she wasn't certain why she was so upset. Was it because they weren't? And that was her fault. She was the one who kept sending River away.

"River has been working with me on getting the house inhabitable again," Edith explained.

"You're not the new owner," he said dismissively.

"Who is?" Jeffries asked with his dispatcher's nosiness.

"I'm not at liberty to say," she said.

"Then how can I be certain you're authorized to be inside the house?" Jeffries asked. "Maybe you and Colton here are the intruders."

River was more right than she'd realized. She shouldn't have called the sheriff. Instead of helping her and River, he was probably going to arrest them.

Knox snorted. "You're kidding, right? Jeffries threatened to take you and Edith to jail?" The sheriff was even more inept than Knox had previously thought. Something had to be done. *He* had to do something. Everybody was right; it was time he threw his hat in the ring for the sheriff's job.

He glanced over at his younger brother as the two searched the new secret room River had found behind the other one off the wine cellar. A small bandage covered the wound on River's forehead.

"Probably would have if Edith hadn't shown him some paperwork she had in her briefcase," River said.

"Did you see it?" Knox asked. Like everyone else, he was curious about the new owner of La Bonne Vie. The person had been careful to conceal their identity. What was the need for secrecy?

River was searching the room more thoroughly than Knox was. Knox was looking for a person—for whoever might have wielded the crowbar the sheriff had left lying on the floor. He hadn't even brought it in for evidence.

The guy was beyond incompetent.

River shrugged. "I didn't try to see it," he said, as if he didn't care for whom Edith worked.

Knox suspected the opposite—that River cared a lot. About Edith...

He had insisted she stay safely upstairs while he and Knox searched the basement again. He must not have believed the sheriff had done a thorough job.

Knox doubted that Bud Jeffries had searched the place at all. But he could see no sign of anyone else inside this room. It wasn't as dusty as the wine cellar had been. But then, it had less stuff in it.

"You didn't see anyone?" Knox asked him again— like he had when he'd joined River and Edith in the ER of Shadow Creek Memorial. She'd brought him there because she'd insisted River get a CT scan.

Edith cared about River, too.

But they were both keeping secrets. She—about her boss. And River...

He was keeping more secret than just what had happened to him during his last deployment. He had another reason for hanging around La Bonne Vie—a reason other than Edith Beaulieu, although Knox suspected she was a big part of it now. Was he just hiding out here while he continued to heal?

River sighed. "Like I told Jeffries, I don't know what the hell happened. I woke up lying on the floor down here next to the crowbar."

"So you don't remember?" The doctor had said he had a concussion but just a slight one. Concussions, however slight, could cause memory loss, though.

"There's nothing to remember," River said. "I opened the door and something hit me."

It had knocked his hat back into the other room, where Edith had found it behind the wine racks. She had shared that with Knox. She hadn't said anything about her fear, but it had been apparent in her big brown eyes. She'd been worried about River—very worried—when she'd found only the hat and not him.

"The sheriff thinks I just walked into something," River bitterly remarked. "Seeing as how I'm half-blind and all…"

"Yeah, you walked into a crowbar," Knox said as he noticed the smear of blood on the metal. "Can't believe he didn't take this for evidence."

"He thinks I fell on it when I walked into the room," River explained. "That I tripped over it or something."

"He doesn't think anyone else was in the house?" Knox asked.

River shook his head and flinched. "There isn't any sign that there was."

"But Edith heard noises…" As she and Knox had waited for River to get the CT scan, she'd filled him in about what had happened.

"Jeffries wrote it off as the wind."

Knox snorted again. Of course the sheriff didn't want any crime in Shadow Creek. Then he might actually have to do his job.

"What do you think it is?" River asked him. "Do you think it's her?"

"Edith?" When Thorne and Mac had showed up at the hospital, they'd exchanged a glance that had reminded Knox of Mac's sister's psychiatric history. They'd seemed more concerned about their young relative than they had even been about River.

"No," River replied and his brow furrowed with confusion. "She didn't hit me with that crowbar. She was upstairs."

"So who do you think hit you?" Knox asked. But his stomach plummeted as he realized who his brother suspected. Of course he had probably put that thought in his head when he'd given him the heads-up the other day. But they'd searched the basement then. Of course they hadn't found the room that River had just found. But he shook his head. "No, she wouldn't risk coming back here."

River had convinced him of that—that it was too risky even for her.

"She's not in Florida," River reminded him.

"Of course not," Knox said. "She's probably in some country with no extradition."

River released a ragged sigh and nodded. "Of course. That makes sense. But then who…"

"Hit you?" Knox asked. He shrugged. "Maybe some reporter snuck in here and didn't want to be arrested for trespassing." He realized the explanation sounded hollow even as he uttered it. But what was the alternative?

That it had been Livia—that she'd knocked out her own son?

He wasn't surprised that she would hurt River. He was surprised that she would risk her freedom by returning to Shadow Creek.

But if she had, she had to be desperate—desperate enough to do anything to remain undetected—even kill. Again.

Chapter 18

Edith Beaulieu was stubborn. River knew that well. He had experienced it firsthand when she'd insisted on bringing him to Shadow Creek Memorial's ER. And when she wouldn't let him help her around the house even after Knox had left and she'd been working.

But this was ridiculous.

"You can't stay here," he said. "It isn't safe."

"Why not?" she asked. "The sheriff searched the house. You and your brother searched the house. Nobody's here."

He touched the bandage on his forehead. "Somebody was…"

She shook her head, and her long hair tumbled around her shoulders. She wore a tank top with shorts, as if she were about to go for a run. But she had taken one earlier while he and Knox had been searching the house.

Still, he didn't believe they'd searched it thoroughly enough. There had to be more secret rooms. They'd found nothing of interest in the new one—at least nothing of interest to River. No papers. No journals…

Livia had kept records. When the FBI had searched the house ten years ago, they'd found some of them, enough evidence to send her to prison. River had already gone through the court transcripts of that evidence, searching for the information he wanted.

But there had been no personal journal among the court exhibits. Surely, Livia would have kept one of those, too. Her personal life had been even more illustrious than her professional one. She would have wanted a record of it, as well.

"Your brother was probably right," Edith said. "That it was a reporter. They've been swarming around the estate."

River doubted it, though. A reporter would have hurled questions at him or shoved a camera in his face, not a crowbar. "It doesn't matter who it was," he said. "It's not safe for you to be here alone."

He stood in the foyer where she'd walked him to the door, insisting he go home to rest. "Come with me," he urged her. "You can stay at Mac's." Or with him in the room above the stables…

In his bed, in his arms…

She shook her head again. "I don't want to stay at Mac's."

He suspected he knew why—that she was worried her uncle thought she was taking after her mother. He'd seen the glance Mac and Thorne had exchanged. But then, they also seemed to believe the sheriff's explanation of his wound—that he'd walked into something.

Maybe that was what Edith believed, too.

"Then get a room in town," he persisted.

"And leave the house empty for that reporter to return?" she asked. "No. I need to stay here."

"Who gives a damn about the house or about the crap left inside?" River asked.

"My boss."

"You would put your life at risk for this guy?" he asked, feeling sick. But his nausea had nothing to do with his concussion and everything to do with jealousy.

She sighed. "You don't understand…"

"Then tell me," he urged her. "Tell me what he means to you." He wanted her to say "nothing." That he meant nothing and River meant everything.

But he had never meant everything to anyone. Not even his own damn mother.

Could it have been she who'd struck him? He would sooner believe it was Livia than that some reporter had figured out a way to sneak inside. But if it was her, there was no way he could leave Edith here alone.

River was too big—too strong—too stubborn—for Edith to be able to throw him out of La Bonne Vie. And if she were honest with herself, she didn't want him to leave.

But once she started being honest with herself, she had to admit something else. That she wanted him.

"Fine," she said, and she slammed shut the door she'd been holding open for him to leave. Then she locked it. Sliding her hand into his, she tugged him across the foyer toward the stairs.

He was strong—too strong for her to pull up the stairs. He stopped at the bottom of them and twirled her around to face him. His brow was furrowed and he stared down at her in confusion. "What's fine?"

He was fine. Too fine for her to ignore any longer.

"You don't want me to stay here alone," she said. "So you're staying with me."

His long, muscular body tensed, and heat flared in his eye. The pupil dilated, swallowing the clear green. "Edith, there's only one bedroom ready and no couch for me to sleep on…"

He was asking what she expected from this evening. She expected danger—far more than she'd faced the night before on her own. Because now it wasn't her life or even her sanity in danger; it was her heart. She was falling for him.

When he'd been missing, she had to face that fact and the disappointment over never having been with him. If he'd stayed missing, she would have lost her chance. And knowing that made her brave enough to take a risk.

"I'm not asking you to sleep on the floor," she told him.

His lips curved into a slight grin. But he must have needed to hear the words because he asked, "Where are you expecting me to sleep?"

She sucked in a breath as her pulse raced away from her. "With me…"

He swung her up in his arms then. And proving that strength, he easily carried her up the stairs and down the hall toward the open doors of the master suite. His steps slowed as he stepped across the threshold and into the room.

Had he changed his mind? Didn't he want her like she wanted him? Or was his concussion bothering him?

She squirmed away from him to slide down his body and regain her feet.

He groaned. But she suspected he was in another kind of physical pain when she felt his erection straining against the fly of his jeans. His hands shook slightly as he cupped her face in his palms and tipped her chin up to meet his gaze. "Are you sure about this?" he asked.

And she understood his hesitation. He was waiting for her to change her mind—as she had too many times before. She stepped back, and she saw the disappointment on his face as he flinched.

Then she tugged her tank top over her head and tossed it onto the floor. Next she shimmied out of her shorts so she stood before him in only her lace bra and panties.

He groaned again. But this time it was her name that left his lips.

He reached for her, skimming his hands over her shoulders, then down her sides to her waist. He pulled her close again as he lowered his head. His mouth covered hers in a passionate kiss that stole away her breath and—just as she'd feared—her sanity.

She lost her mind to desire. And as it overwhelmed her, she clutched at his T-shirt, hauling it up and over his head. He wasn't wearing his hat. Maybe because it would have fit too tightly against the bump on his head, or maybe because of the blood smeared on it. She ran her fingers over his short hair; it tickled her palms.

Then she skimmed her hands down to his shoulders. They were so broad. Muscles rippled in them and his arms as he lifted her again. He carried her to bed. And as he laid her on it, he followed her down. The dog tags dangled from around his neck, the metal warm from his body, bumping against her breasts. He reached up to pull them off.

But she caught them in her hand and slid them around to his back. She didn't want him to take them off; she instinctively knew that they were too important to him. And because they were important to him, they were to her, as well.

He stared at her for a moment as if unable to believe that she was real. Then he kissed her, his lips nibbling before his tongue stroked across hers. He deepened the kiss, making love to her mouth like she wanted him to make love to her body.

She wriggled beneath him as the ache intensified inside her.

He pulled back, but only enough to unclasp her bra and toss it aside. Then his mouth moved to her breasts. He teased one nipple with his tongue while his fingers toyed with the other.

She moaned and raked her nails over his shoulders. She tried tugging him up her body. But she didn't want just his kiss again. She wanted all of him. She stretched, trying to reach his belt buckle. And her fingers skimmed over his fly.

He groaned against her breast. Then he pulled away and stood up.

Had he changed his mind?

Was this—was she—not what he wanted?

But before she could protest, he reached for his belt buckle. He unclasped it and unzipped his jeans before pushing them down his legs along with his boxers. Then he stood naked before her.

And she gasped as desire overwhelmed her. He was so big—everywhere. His erection jutted toward her. She reached out a trembling hand for it, but before she could close her fingers around him, he jerked back and shook his head.

"No," he told her, his voice gruff. "It's been a long time for me…"

So that should make him want to hurry. It was why she wanted to hurry. Because it had been so long and maybe because she was afraid that she would come to her senses.

But he refused to hurry. Even as he rejoined her on the bed, he took his time. He kissed and caressed every inch of her skin before finally moving down to the core of her desire for him. Her body ached and throbbed.

He pulled her panties down and dropped them off the bed. Then he made love to her with his mouth. He drove her to madness again with his lips and with his tongue, teasing and stroking her. The tension inside her wound tightly until it snapped. She rose off the bed and cried out as pleasure overwhelmed her. But despite the release, she still felt empty. She needed him inside her.

He was gone again, though. And she realized why when she heard the tear of a packet. He donned a condom before joining her again—really joining her. His erection nudged her core before easing inside her.

And finally that emptiness was filled. He filled her and then some, with his size and his passion. He kissed and caressed her even as he moved inside her, thrusting gently in and out.

It wasn't enough—not as the tension built again in

her body. She clutched at him, kissing him as passionately as he kissed her. She nipped at his lips and his tongue. And she wrapped her legs around his lean waist, matching his rhythm. They moved together—each desperate for release.

But he waited until she came again, screaming his name, before he joined her. His body tensed, then shuddered, and he shouted with his release. He shouted her name, "Edith!"

It had never sounded sexy until it escaped his lips with a guttural groan of pure joy. Satiated with pleasure, her body went limp. Even her mind, which had been so full of thoughts and fear, slowed. For the first time in longer than she could remember—in maybe forever—Edith relaxed.

River must have left her. She heard water running. But no pipes clanged. Nothing scraped. The water shut off. Then he was back in her bed. And she was back in his arms.

She moved naturally against him, settling her head against his shoulder as she stroked his chest. He'd moved his dog tags back around to the front. She toyed with the metal, running her fingertips along the imprint of his name before she moved to the next tag. But it wasn't his name on that one.

"Henry," he murmured.

That was the name she'd heard him call out when he'd had that nightmare. "Why do you have his?" she asked.

"Because he had no one else to take them."

Henry must have been one of the men he'd lost on that mission—someone who'd had no family, no one to turn to. She knew what that was like. After her father had died, she'd felt so alone.

So scared…

But she wasn't alone or afraid now. She had never felt as safe as she did in River Colton's arms. To feel that way about a man she barely knew, a man she didn't completely trust, was more dangerous than staying alone at La Bonne Vie.

But she couldn't make him leave. She didn't want to—because she knew, no matter how satiated she was, she would want him again.

Declan cursed as he read the most recent report on *Everything's Blogger in Texas*. A Possible Break-In at La Bonne Vie.

What the hell was going on at the estate and why hadn't Edith called him about it?

He shouldn't have left her alone there. It was obviously more dangerous than he'd realized. He'd thought the only danger she'd been in was falling for River Colton. He'd believed her statement that the wine racks falling over had been an accident. Now he knew there was more going on than he'd feared. His hand shook slightly as he reached for his cell and punched in her contact.

It rang just a couple of times before a voice answered. "Hello?" It sounded husky with sleep but it was also deep and very masculine.

A man had answered Edith's cell phone.

"Who the hell are you?" he demanded to know, even as he was afraid that he already did. He was even more afraid for Edith now.

Chapter 19

River hadn't been sleeping when the phone rang. He'd been watching Edith sleep as he held her, making sure she was safe. He'd also been listening intently for the noises she'd heard the night before. But he'd heard nothing until her cell had begun to ring.

He'd answered it quickly so she wouldn't awaken. Maybe he'd answered it too quickly because now he had no idea what to say. This had to be the man—her boss—who hated Coltons as much or more than Sheriff Jeffries did.

Jeffries was probably just jealous of what he imagined was their wealth and privilege. What was this man's reason?

"Who is this?" River asked, turning the question around on the caller.

The guy said nothing for a long moment, but River

could feel the tension and resentment in the silence. Then he demanded, "Put Edith on the line."

"She's sleeping," he replied. But she wasn't anymore.

Her body had tensed, and she lifted her head from his chest. The light from the cell phone cast a glow in the dark bedroom. And he could see how her eyes widened with fear.

Was she afraid to find him in her bed? She'd invited him to stay.

No. She seemed more afraid to find him on her cell phone. "That's mine," she said with a gasp, as she must have realized who her caller was.

Was she used to him calling her this late at night? In the middle of the night?

River held on to the phone even as she reached for it.

"Give it to me," she said.

Reluctantly he handed it over. But she said nothing to her caller. Instead she spoke to him, "I need to take this," she said. "In private…"

He got the message. He was no longer wanted. Rolling out of bed, he grabbed up his clothes from the floor. He didn't even bother getting dressed, just brought them all with him as he stepped into the hall.

He'd give her all the damn privacy she wanted— because now he wanted some of his own. He didn't like the way her boss made him feel.

Didn't like being jealous of a man he'd never met. But he worried that this unnamed boss of Edith's meant more to her than River ever would.

Could he blame her? The guy was obviously rich and successful—while River had lost his career along with his eye. He'd lost his identity during that explosion and when he'd come home to learn his father wasn't the man he'd always thought he was.

Who the hell was he?

Until River knew, he had nothing to offer Edith.

Edith stared after River with a mixture of longing and regret. He was so damn good-looking. Muscles had rippled even in his ass as he'd walked away from her. Naked and proud.

"Edith!" Declan shouted her name from the phone, bringing her back to her senses.

"Yes…" she murmured. She'd been so deeply asleep that she struggled to awake even now.

"Who the hell was that or do I even need to ask?"

"Obviously you don't," she replied.

"River Colton?" He uttered the name as a question, anyway, his deep voice echoing hollowly in her ear with the sound of disappointment and betrayal.

She drew in a deep breath and sat up against the pillow. Even though Declan couldn't see her, she pulled the blankets up to her neck. She felt exposed in a way she never had before. But Declan couldn't know that he'd caught them in bed together. Or could he?

"Edith," Declan called out again as if worried that she'd hung up on him.

Maybe she should have. It was late. She wasn't on the clock right now. But then, as his executive assistant, she was never off the clock. That had never bothered her before—because she'd had nothing for work to disrupt before.

"Yes," she said.

His breath hissed through the phone in a sigh of

shock. He must have taken her reply as affirmation that River had answered her phone.

"What the hell is he doing there at this hour?" he demanded to know.

Sick of being on the defensive, she asked, "What the hell are you doing calling at this hour?"

Another breath hissed through the phone. She'd obviously shocked him again.

She'd shocked herself, as well. She had never spoken to him that way before—not just because he was her boss but also because he was her brother. He had protected her in that foster home. She owed him.

"I just saw the report about there being a break-in at La Bonne Vie," he replied. "I was worried about you, apparently with good reason."

She felt a pang of guilt. "I'm sorry," she murmured. "But you should know better than to believe that blog."

"So there was no break-in?"

"No." The sheriff had assured her that there were no signs of forced entry. So how had the news of a break-in leaked to the media?

Unless the person who'd been in the house had leaked it? Or had the dispatcher? Edith's money was on the dispatcher, who'd probably been paid for the report. *Everything's Blogger* had paid an old boyfriend of Leonor's for scoop on the Coltons. Thorne had told her that; that was why he'd limited the guest list for his and Maggie's wedding. He had wanted only people they could trust at their special event.

Edith had been there. She'd even asked Declan to be her plus one. But, predictably, he had refused.

Why?

"There's something you're not telling me," Declan

said with suspicion and anger. "What's going on, Edith? Why are you with River Colton?"

Because she was falling for him. But she couldn't admit that even to herself yet. She didn't want to face her fears.

"He's protecting me," Edith said.

"And if there was no break-in, what do you need protecting from?" Declan asked.

Edith heard it again. First the clanging noise. Then a scraping noise. And she shivered. "I don't know what's going on in this house," she said. "And I didn't want to be alone here."

"Why River?" Declan asked. "If you need protection, why didn't you tell me and I could have sent out a security team?"

"You didn't want me to hire a handyman," she reminded him. "I doubted you wanted security guards hanging around, too."

"Then what about your uncle?" Declan asked. "Why didn't you turn to him?"

Maybe it was the promise she'd made to her mother all those years ago. Merrilee hadn't wanted her brother to know how sick she was. She'd insisted Edith tell the social workers that they had no family. That it was just the two of them.

But it had never been just the two of them. Merrilee had never been there for her after her father's death.

"I don't know," she replied.

"If you had to turn to a Colton, why not Thorne?" he asked. "He's your cousin. Why *River*?" His deep voice reverberated with resentment of the other man.

Had they ever met? With River being gone as a Marine for so many years, she doubted it.

"Why do you have a problem with River?" she asked. "Why do you have a problem with *any* of the Coltons?"

"Because I don't trust them," Declan said. "And neither should you. I don't want any of them in La Bonne Vie."

She flinched as she realized that a few of them had been there. River. Thorne. Knox.

She drew in a breath, bracing herself for the admission she should have made days ago. "River's been working here."

A curse slipped out of Declan now. But he sounded almost calm when he asked, "Why?"

"I needed someone to make some necessary repairs around here—"

"No," Declan interrupted her. "I'm not asking why you hired him. I'm asking why he wants to work there."

"You know why," she said. "You read that blog." She couldn't understand why a man as busy as Declan would waste his time on it. "You know River was hurt on his last deployment. He's no longer a Marine."

"He's not a handyman, either," Declan pointed out.

"He needed something to do." And she…she'd needed River. She still did.

"He can work for your uncle on his ranch. Or for his sister-in-law if he wants to do construction. He has another reason for wanting to work at La Bonne Vie."

Warmth flooded her heart. Was it her? Had he just wanted to work with her?

But when he'd asked for the job, he'd seemed more interested in the house than in her. Did he have an ulterior motive?

She heard another scraping sound and shivered.

"What reason could he have?" she asked. And she actually hoped Declan had an answer for her. She wanted to know.

"I don't know" was his disappointing reply. "Maybe he's looking for something in the house, something he thinks his mother left behind…"

She shivered again as she realized Declan could be right. Had River just been using her to search the house?

"What could she have left?" she asked.

Declan sighed. "Who knows? Money? The FBI never found much, so she must have stashed it somewhere."

Of course Declan would think about money. It mattered most to him, too.

"I'm worried about you," he said. And she knew that she mattered to him, too. There was affection along with the concern in his voice. "I don't want you staying there alone."

"I'm not—"

"And I don't want River Colton anywhere near you or that house anymore," he continued. "You need to fire him."

"Declan," she said. "You don't know that you're right about him."

"You know," he told her, calling her on the doubts he must have heard in her voice. "You know I'm right."

She was afraid that she did. Or was she just looking for another excuse to push River away so she didn't fall irrevocably in love with him?

"And even if you're too stubborn to admit that," he continued, "you know I'm the owner of La Bonne Vie now. This is my call. You fire River Colton tonight."

First she had to find him.

Where had he gone?

He was at La Bonne Vie. Knox knew where River was even without calling him. He'd talked to Mac earlier. River hadn't told him where he was, either, but they'd both known he was with Edith.

He was protecting her.

But who was protecting River?

That crowbar could have killed him had the blow been just a little bit harder. Who'd swung it at him? The reporter Knox had suggested? Or their mother?

Could she hurt her own child?

He stared down at his. The sleeping boy looked happy, his lips curved slightly as if he dreamed happy dreams. Knox was glad. Right after it had happened, his son had had a couple nightmares about his kidnapping. But now it was as if he hardly remembered it.

Knox would never forget it—never forget his son being used as leverage against Livia. Was that what someone was doing with River? Hurting him to get back at her?

Sure, she'd brought Cody's kidnapper to her kind of justice. But that hadn't been out of any sense of grandmotherly love or affection. She wasn't capable of love for anyone but herself.

Not wanting his tension to disturb his son, Knox backed out of the boy's room and closed the door. But he wasn't alone in the hall. Allison leaned against the wall, watching him like he'd watched Cody.

She looked so beautiful that his heart swelled inside his chest. Her long, dark blond hair lay in waves around her shoulders, which were bare but for the thin straps of her nightgown.

"Are you okay?" she asked, her hazel eyes warm with concern. And love.

He knew better than to lie to her. So he shook his head.

"What's wrong?"

"I'm worried."

She gasped. "About Cody? Do you think anyone's going to try to hurt him again?"

He drew his wife into his arms and held her close. "Nobody will hurt our son again."

"How can you be sure?" she asked.

He cupped her face in his palms and stared deeply into her eyes. "Because I'll make certain of it."

"How?" she asked him.

She was a stubborn woman. He already knew that. But he suspected she was getting at something else with her questions. He'd been struggling at how to bring up the subject. But now he knew he hadn't had to wait until the perfect moment. In fact, he knew he shouldn't have waited at all.

"Because I'm going to run for sheriff," he replied.

A smile curved her lips and she nodded. "It's about damn time. Shadow Creek needs you."

"The voters might not see it that way," he cautioned her. "They might only see a Colton." And because of that, they probably wouldn't trust him.

"They'll see a former Texas Ranger who is all about honor and duty and the law," she assured him. "There's no way you will lose."

He smiled now. "Not with you on my side."

"Shadow Creek isn't the only one who needs you,"

she said as she grabbed his hand and steered him down the hall toward their bedroom. "I need you."

He needed her, too. He also needed to make sure his family was never in danger again. But he had a bad feeling that River was.

Chapter 20

He didn't have much time. River knew that. The minute Edith had told him she needed privacy for her call he'd headed down to the basement. This was probably his last chance to look around—given that he had no doubt her boss would order her to fire him.

Was the man jealous? Did he have reason to be?

River's stomach lurched with his own jealousy. He had only himself to blame. He'd known right away that Edith's employer was more than just her boss to her. They had some other kind of relationship, some kind that River would never have with her.

At least he'd had tonight. But making love with her—knowing how incredible it could be between them—would only make it harder, would make him miss her more if it was over. Was it over?

Maybe his search was. Now that he knew where the

other mechanisms to open the secret doors had been hidden, it was easy to find them in the stone walls. He'd found more secret rooms. His mother had had a maze of them built into the basement.

The FBI must have found some of them, as well, because they looked as though they'd already been searched. River picked up papers and books from the floor and thumbed through them. Nothing looked like a journal. If the FBI had found it, he doubted they would have left it behind. But maybe Livia had written it in some kind of secret code that they hadn't understood. So he studied the pages with more interest—so much that he hadn't heard her approach until she gasped.

"There are more of these rooms?"

He glanced up to find Edith standing in the doorway of the last room he'd found. She'd dressed in yoga pants and a sweatshirt. But he could see her as she'd been when she'd undressed, revealing her lacy underwear.

His muscles tensed as desire overwhelmed him. Yes, making love with her had only made it worse, had only made him want her more.

"Yes," he said. "There are more rooms." He suspected even more than he'd found.

"Did you know they were here?" she asked.

"I knew the FBI had found some," he said. "That's where they discovered the evidence the federal prosecutors used to convict her."

Edith glanced around the room and shivered, as if it were a crime scene. Knowing his mother, maybe it had been. Who knew how many people she'd killed?

River doubted the authorities knew.

"You don't think they found them all?"

He was pretty sure they hadn't. But he just shrugged.

"Is that why you wanted to work here?" she asked. "So you could search for these rooms?"

"Edith…" He stepped closer to her, but she stepped back—out of that secret room and into the one before it, the one in which he'd been hit with the crowbar.

"I suspected you had a reason for wanting to be here," she said. "I even suspected you were looking for something, so I shouldn't be surprised." But it was clear that she was.

He said nothing as he internally debated whether or not to tell her the truth. He wasn't certain if she would understand or if she would be even angrier with him for not being honest with her from the beginning.

"Is it money?" she asked. "Is that what you're trying to find?"

He gasped now. "What?"

"Did your mother have money hidden in the house?"

He shrugged. "Probably."

Knowing Livia, he would believe it. If she had returned to Shadow Creek, that might be why. He hoped like hell she wasn't back, though. He glanced around the dimly lit room. He hadn't found anyone in the rooms he'd just discovered, though. But if there were more, she could be hiding in one of them.

"So that's why you wanted to work here," she said. "You wanted access to the house. Access to that money…"

Her assumption stung his pride hard. But he didn't defend himself. He wasn't looking for money, but he had been looking for something. If he told her the truth now, she wouldn't feel any less betrayed, though. He would only be proving to her that he had a motive for wanting to work for her.

He didn't want to hurt her. But he suspected it was too late for that. He should have been honest with her from the beginning. Of course, he doubted that she would have let him anywhere near the house—or her—if he had. And he couldn't regret what had happened between them.

He only regretted that it was unlikely to ever happen again.

Edith waited for River to deny what she was saying. She waited for him to explain what he was doing in the basement—in the secret rooms. But he said nothing. He just stared at her with regret.

A pang struck her heart. Declan was right. She had been a fool to trust River. He had definitely been keeping something from her. She wasn't sure it was about hidden money. But he had some secret he wasn't sharing with her.

Along with the regret, she saw the guilt on his handsome face. "So you were just using me…"

He shook his head now and flinched. The concussion must have still been bothering him. But not enough that he hadn't risked getting another one by coming downstairs alone. "I wasn't using you," he insisted.

"Working for me was just an excuse to get access to the house."

"*Working* for you was," he admitted. "But what else we did…" He gestured toward the ceiling, the floor joists above were exposed here. The room hadn't been completely finished. "I wasn't using you."

She might have actually been using him—to protect her from her fears. To free her from the desire she'd felt for him. But finding him down here, searching these secret rooms, that freed her. She was in no danger of falling for someone she couldn't trust.

"You're not working for me anymore," she informed him.

"Your boss told you to fire me?" he asked.

Declan had. But that had nothing to do with what she was doing now.

"It doesn't matter what he said," she informed River. "I don't want you working for me anymore."

"I understand," he said. "You feel betrayed."

"Because you betrayed me," she said.

He stepped closer. "No, Edith, I would never purposely hurt you."

She stepped back. "You didn't hurt me." She ignored that aching pain in her chest, in her heart. "I would have had to care for you, for you to be able to hurt me."

He flinched. "Edith…"

She glanced up at the ceiling now. "That wasn't about anything but sex."

"Just sex?" he repeated skeptically. "That's all that was?" He moved closer to her yet.

This time she didn't step back. She couldn't betray how he affected her even now—after she knew the truth. Her pulse quickened and her skin heated, her body flushing with desire for him. How could she still want him?

She nodded. "Of course. I don't have time for anything else. I don't have time for relationships. And I don't have time for you. You need to leave."

He leaned down, putting his face close to hers—as if he intended to kiss her. She held her breath, waiting to see if he'd try it.

She wasn't sure what she would do. She was afraid that she actually might kiss him back. He was so handsome, so sexy. She could almost taste his breath, taste the rich, distinctive flavor that was River. Her pulse quickened even more, and her skin tingled.

But he stepped away from her this time. "I'll leave," he said. "But you need to leave, as well. You can't stay here alone."

"Why not?" she asked. "Are you going to sneak inside the minute I turn my back?"

Maybe that had been him she'd heard the night she hadn't been able to sleep because of all the noises. The noises she'd heard again tonight when he'd been opening up all these secret rooms.

He flinched again as if she'd struck him. "You're not safe here. I don't believe those racks accidentally fell over on you that night. And I don't think you do, either."

She remembered the shadow against the stone wall she'd seen just before the racks had toppled. And her blood chilled with fear and dread.

"And I didn't hit myself with that crowbar," he said.

That was true. Even if he'd been searching the rooms, someone else must have been inside one of them—someone who'd struck him.

"Did you really not see anything?" she asked.

Or did he have an accomplice who'd turned on him? Someone also searching for money or whatever else Livia might have left in the house.

"Do you think I'm protecting someone?" he asked.

"Are you?"

"You," he replied. "You're the only one I want to protect."

But he couldn't save her from the person who could hurt her the most—because he was that person. Despite her best efforts to fight her feelings for him, she had begun to fall. That was why it hurt so much to realize he'd only been using her.

She blinked back the tears that had started to well in her eyes. She had never cried in front of the bigger kids in the foster home; she hadn't wanted to give them the satisfaction or reveal her weakness. But their teasing and their tricks had never affected her like this. And then she'd had Declan to defend and support her.

He would have no sympathy for her now. He'd warned her about the Coltons and she hadn't listened to him.

"Promise me you won't stay here alone," River implored her.

For a moment her heart warmed, as she allowed herself to believe that he might actually care about her.

Then he added, "Stay at your uncle's."

And she didn't know if he cared or if he just wanted her out of the house and out of his way so he could search without her interrupting him.

"It's none of your business what I do," she informed him. "And you no longer have any business being here. You're fired, so now you're trespassing."

"Edith—"

"Leave now or I will call Sheriff Jeffries," she threatened him. "I have a feeling he would be happy to lock you up." Maybe any Colton would suffice with the Shadow Creek lawman.

Maybe it was the threat of jail that got to him. But River sighed with resignation and walked past her. He stopped only a few steps behind her, though, because she could almost feel the heat of his body yet—like she'd felt it while she'd slept in his arms. She'd felt so satiated and safe then. But then, she had been foolish enough to trust him.

"I'm sorry, Edith," he said, his voice gruff with regret and something else. "I never meant to hurt you."

She'd already denied that he had. But he must have known she was lying. Maybe he'd seen her fighting back the tears. She waited until she heard him walk away before she allowed one to spill over and slide down her cheek.

He had gotten too damn close. Livia tightened her grasp on the gun she'd been holding. If he'd found this room, she would have had to shoot him. It didn't matter that he was her son. Hell, she should have finished him off the other day. But the one blow hadn't roused much suspicion. That fool Jeffries had believed River had just stumbled into something or tripped and fallen.

She suspected even Knox had been willing to believe that, rather than entertain the notion that Mommy Dearest had returned to Shadow Creek. Her sons had nothing to worry about, though—at least not now that River had been fired and would no longer be poking around the basement of La Bonne Vie. But now someone else was poking.

She heard footsteps on the other side of the fake stone walls. Then someone began to scrape at it. That damn woman…

Edith Beaulieu had been a problem since she'd first started working on La Bonne Vie. It was past time that Livia deal with that problem—once and for all.

Chapter 21

Maybe Edith would stay at Mac's if he was gone. But River had no place else to go. Yet.

So he made a call.

"Howard Security Services," a male voice answered.

"Not all that inventive," River remarked. "I figured Leonor would make you come up with something more prosaic than just your last name."

Joshua Howard chuckled. "I was actually just trying that out. And yes, of course, my lovely fiancée is trying to come up with something more creative."

As a museum curator, Leonor had a flare for the dramatic. "I'm sure she'll come up with something awesome." He had confidence in his oldest sister.

"The name isn't the only thing I need," Josh said. "I need employees."

"So the job offer's still open?"

"Of course," Josh said. "You interested now?"

River drew in a deep breath. "Yes. I'll take it." Because of his injury, he could no longer be the kind of Marine he'd once been. But he could still protect people—just not the person he most wanted to protect. Edith.

"I thought you had a job," Josh said. "At La Bonne Vie…"

"Not anymore." She had fired him a few days ago. But he'd hoped she would change her mind, so he'd stayed at the ranch, working for Mac and Thorne and working with Shadow. And all the while, he'd waited for her to realize that she would need him to help her finish up the house for her boss's visit and that he hadn't been using her.

But he had been. He'd wanted to get into those secret rooms. He'd wanted to search for those secrets.

Now he didn't even care who the hell his father was. He'd lost something much more important to him than his identity; he'd lost Edith.

Not that he'd ever really had her. For every step she'd taken toward him and what they could have together, she had taken three steps back. And after that night they'd shared such incredible passion, he should have known she would push him far away.

Not that he hadn't given her a reason.

"I heard you got hurt on the job," Josh said. "You okay now?"

His head no longer throbbed and the swelling on his forehead had gone down. But he was hurting like hell—in his chest. He felt like he had a gaping hole where his heart had once been.

"Yeah, yeah, I'm fine," he assured his new boss. Or potential new boss. "So am I hired?"

"Yes, of course," Josh replied. "How soon can you move to Austin?"

"Right away," River said. "There's nothing keeping me here in Shadow Creek." Not anymore.

Edith had that same eerie sensation she always had at La Bonne Vie. That she wasn't alone.

Of course now she had a reason. Every time she glanced up from her inventory, she found either her uncle or her cousin watching over her. Sometimes they both showed up—like today—under the guise of bringing her lunch.

Her stomach roiled at the smell of the pizza they'd brought. She hadn't been eating. Not since she'd fired River. She hadn't been sleeping, either.

The last good rest she'd gotten had been in his arms, with her head on his chest, because she'd felt safe then. She'd been such a fool.

And because she hadn't wanted to be reminded of that night, of what they'd done in that bed, she had taken a room in town again. But it didn't matter. Even when she wasn't at La Bonne Vie, she couldn't escape the memories of River.

The way he'd looked, bare chested, sun gleaming on his sweat-slick skin and glinting off the dog tags he wore around his neck. The way he'd tasted, his lips moving over hers. The way he'd touched her...

She shivered.

"Are you cold?" Uncle Mac asked. Of course he wouldn't have missed her shiver—not with as closely as he'd been watching her.

Did he and Thorne think she was going to get sick, just like her mother had?

Did they know how she felt about River?

It wasn't as if Edith had actually fallen for him. At least not completely…

"I'm fine," she assured him. She turned toward her cousin, who watched her just as intently. "You two don't need to keep checking up on me."

Thorne nodded as if he agreed with her. "It wasn't my idea."

She turned toward Uncle Mac, who shook his head. "Not mine, either."

"Then who?" Declan certainly wouldn't have asked them. He didn't want any Coltons in La Bonne Vie again. He had hired a security guard to be with her whenever she was at the estate. But the guy's silent presence had unnerved her. So she'd fired him and when Declan had protested, she'd admitted that she hadn't heard or seen anything suspicious around the estate since she'd fired River. He'd refrained from saying "I told you so" and from sending another security guard.

"River asked us to check on you," Thorne replied. "He doesn't want you to be alone up here. He doesn't think it's safe."

Then where was he? She wanted to ask. But she didn't want to betray how much she cared and how badly she missed him. She snorted. "I'm perfectly safe now."

Now that she had fired him. That he couldn't use her anymore. Use her for what, though?

She hadn't found any more secret rooms in addition to the ones he'd already found. And the only one that had contained anything of value had been that first one, with vintage wine bottles. He'd only touched one of those—the one he'd brought upstairs for them to share.

And when she'd thrown him out of La Bonne Vie, he hadn't appeared to have stuffed any money or valuables in his pockets. Whatever he'd been looking for, she doubted he'd found it. So why hadn't he been back?

"And if he's so worried," she continued, as her temper flared, "why hasn't he checked on me himself?" Because he knew there was no actual threat in the house. The only real threat had been her falling for him.

Mac chuckled. "Because he doesn't think it would be safe, not with you being as angry as you are with him."

Thorne grinned. "I believe there was some mention of your threatening to call Sheriff Jeffries on him."

Heat rushed to her face. "It wasn't an idle threat," she admitted.

"Why are you so angry with him?" Thorne asked.

Edith doubted River had told his brother and Mac everything. "He wasn't working for me because he really wanted to work on this house."

"I didn't think he had a sudden desire to become a handyman, either," Thorne said.

"Then you know he was searching the place?"

Thorne narrowed his pale brown eyes. "Searching the place for what?"

She shrugged. "Something your mother must have hidden here—in one of her secret rooms."

Thorne and Mac exchanged a glance. Did they have some idea what he'd been looking for?

"What is it?" she asked.

Thorne shrugged now. "I think you're the reason he wanted to work here, Edith. He cares about you."

"That's why he's asked us to check on you so much," Uncle Mac said. "And even if you wouldn't call the sheriff on him, he wouldn't be able to check on you himself now."

Her heartbeat paused for a moment before resuming at a faster rate. "Why not?"

Had something happened to him?

Had he not fully recovered from his concussion?

"Leonor's fiancé, Josh Howard, is starting a security business in Austin," Thorne said. "He'd offered River a job a while ago, but he'd turned him down then."

He had mentioned the job to her, but he hadn't seemed all that interested in taking it. She'd wondered why then.

So she asked them now, "Why?" River was so strong and smart; he would make an excellent security guard.

"Because he was working for you," Thorne said. "Now that you fired him, he accepted the job."

"He's moving to Austin?" Was he doing that just for the job or to get away from his family's pity or from her?

She remembered that along with the guilt, he had also looked hurt—that she would think he was just after money. But if not that, what?

"His assignments could bring him anywhere, though," Uncle Mac added. He glanced around the kitchen. "Maybe even back here."

She furrowed her brow in confusion. "How?"

"Since he's so worried about your safety here at La Bonne Vie, maybe you should be his first client."

"You think I should hire River to be my bodyguard?" She chuckled, although it sounded hollow even to her. But then, she felt hollow, as well. The emptiness inside her had only been filled one night—by River.

Ignoring their nods, she gestured around the quiet kitchen. "I don't need a bodyguard. Surely, you two realize that now. Every time you've showed up to check on me, there's been nothing happening around here. No noises. No shadows in the dark..."

Maybe all that had been River. Because since he'd left, nothing had happened that had unsettled Edith. But since he'd left, there were also no kisses. No caresses.

Father and son exchanged another glance. This one she easily interpreted. They agreed with her.

"You two have a ranch to run," she reminded them. Then she turned toward her cousin. "And you have a baby on the way. You should be sticking close to your wife."

Thorne's eyes filled with love and affection for his bride.

"She needs you," Edith said. "I don't. I can take care of myself. I've been doing it a long time."

Mac's eyes darkened for a moment with regret. And she felt bad for making him feel guilt. So she hugged him. "It's fine. I'm fine. I'm stronger and more independent because of it."

She didn't need a man. Any man. She could take care of herself.

Mac hugged her back before pulling away. "She's right," he told his son. "She can take care of herself."

"Tell River..." She trailed off as she thought of all the things she wanted to tell him. But when she'd fired him, she'd said everything.

Goodbye.

They must have just assumed she wanted them to tell River she could take care of herself because they nodded as if they would. Then they headed out the door toward their trucks. The engines rumbled as they started them and drove away.

They could have only been gone a few moments when she heard another sound. It was the clanging of something metallic and then the scraping noise. Now she knew what that sound was: someone going in and out of those secret rooms.

Someone was downstairs.

River?

Had he come back to search the basement one more time before he moved to Austin? Her pulse quickened with anger and, if she were being honest, excitement at the thought of seeing him.

She had missed him so much. Even as angry as she was with him, she wanted to see him. But she was no fool. Just in case it wasn't him, she grabbed her canister of pepper spray. Then she headed downstairs to investigate.

No. She didn't need a bodyguard or any man at all. But she wanted one.

She wanted River.

Where the hell was she?

Declan hadn't told her he was coming. But he'd expected her to be at the house. Hell, her car was parked outside by that fountain where moments before two trucks had been parked, as well. He'd waited for them to leave before he'd driven through the gates.

He had expected to see River Colton driving one

of those trucks. He'd almost wanted to see the man in person—instead of just on the front page of the *Everything's Blogger* website. But Thorne had driven one and Joseph "Mac" Mackenzie the other. He'd recognized them from the blog, as well, and from the photographs Edith had of them.

He couldn't be angry with her over allowing her uncle and her cousin in the house. They were her family. At least she had some.

He didn't anymore, thanks to Livia Colton.

Except for Edith. He considered her family. She was like his little sister.

That was why he had showed up early for his visit— because he was worried about her. River Colton had gotten to her, no matter how much she might deny it.

And maybe La Bonne Vie had gotten to her, as well.

Declan shouldn't have let her fire the security guard. It wasn't safe for her to work alone. She'd been hurt there. There had been reports of an intruder.

"Edith?" he called out. His voice echoed hollowly in the empty house, bouncing off the marble floors and high plaster ceilings of the foyer.

He looked at the elegant staircase where so many photographs of Livia Colton had been taken as she'd stood above her guests, looking down on all of them like they were her minions.

So many men had been. Mindless fools she'd manipulated to do her bidding. Who was she manipulating now that she was able to continue to elude the authorities? Would she never serve out her sentence?

Anger coursed through Declan, as it did every time he let himself think of her and the injustice of it all. But along with the anger, he had fear. Not of Livia.

He was no longer the seven-year-old kid whose life she had selfishly destroyed. She couldn't hurt him anymore. But she could hurt someone else—the only other person he cared about.

"Edith?" he shouted again as he walked through the house and headed into the kitchen that smelled of the pizza sitting on the table nearly untouched. Pulling his cell from the pocket of his suit coat, he clicked her contact information.

Something vibrated along the kitchen countertop near where he stood. Her cell phone sat next to her purse on the stainless steel counter.

And her car was in the drive.

She was here. But where?

What the hell had happened to her?

Chapter 22

"You're still here?"

River looked up from the duffel bag he was packing. Mac leaned against the doorjamb of the stairwell leading down to the stables below. "Are you anxious to get rid of me?" he asked the older man. "Have I overstayed my welcome?"

"Never," Mac assured him. "You just took this job so quickly that I thought you were anxious to start it."

He shook his head. "Josh doesn't even have the company completely up and running yet."

"Then what's your hurry to leave?"

River sighed. "Because I have no reason to stay." Not with Edith being unable to forgive him.

Mac turned at the sound of footsteps on the stairs, then he backed into the room as a tall man stepped through the doorway behind him. He glanced back at River. "A friend of yours?"

River furrowed his brow with confusion as he tried to recognize the man. "No…"

"Can we help you?" Mac asked the stranger.

"I have some questions regarding Edith Beaulieu."

A pang struck River's heart as he recognized the deep voice. "You're her boss," he murmured. But they were more than that to each other; they'd both admitted it. River studied him and realized most women would find him attractive. He was tall and broad-shouldered with dark brown hair and green eyes. He looked vaguely familiar to River, like someone he used to know…

The guy stared at him, as well. Since he'd been disfigured, River was used to people staring. But something about this guy's scrutiny bothered him. It was like he was being assessed and found wanting.

"What's your name?" River asked the stranger.

Since the guy was so hell-bent on remaining anonymous, River didn't actually expect him to answer. But he did. "Declan Sinclair."

Mac gasped as if he recognized the name.

The name and the man meant nothing to River.

"What are you doing here?" River asked him. "Edith already fired me—just like you told her to."

"You had no business being in La Bonne Vie to begin with," Declan told him.

"And you have no business here," River said.

Mac glanced back and forth between the two of them as if they were two dogs circling each other to fight and he was worried he would get caught—and bitten—in the middle.

"Edith is my business," Declan replied.

"If you came by to warn me to stay away from her,

you're wasting your time." River gestured at his packed duffel bag. "I'm already leaving town."

Declan nodded as if he approved. But his jaw remained clenched, a muscle twitching in his cheek. He had something else to say, obviously, but it appeared stuck in his throat.

Obviously uncomfortable, Mac moved around Sinclair and headed toward the stairwell. "I'll leave you two alone for now…"

But Declan reached out and caught his arm. Maybe he didn't want to be alone with River.

River wasn't particularly eager to be alone with him, either. He wasn't afraid of him. Despite the guy's size, he could take him apart—if he wanted. Once a Marine, always a Marine. He hadn't forgotten anything the Corps had taught him.

"When did you see Edith last?" Declan asked Mac.

"Just a little while ago," he replied. "My son and I brought her lunch."

Declan nodded like Mac had passed some quiz. Then he turned away from him, as if dismissing the older man from his own property. Mac shrugged before heading off down the stairs.

But tension filled River and it wasn't just because he was now alone with the vaguely familiar-looking stranger. "Why are you asking about Edith? Haven't you seen her yet?"

Declan shook his head.

And a chill chased down River's back. Even though he doubted it, he asked the question. "You came here before going to La Bonne Vie?"

That muscle twitched again before Sinclair answered. "No."

"You haven't seen her?"

"I couldn't find her," he admitted. "Her car is in the driveway. Her purse and her phone are on the kitchen counter, but she's nowhere to be found."

River's gut clenched as fear overwhelmed him. But he shook his head, refusing to jump to the worst conclusion. "She could have gone for a run," he suggested. "You know how she does that to relieve stress."

Declan nodded. "Yeah, yeah…" But then he shook his head. "She always takes her phone, though. She uses the running app on it to keep track of her time and distance."

River knew that, as well. He headed toward the door, shoving past Declan, who slightly blocked his way.

"Where the hell are you going?"

"To La Bonne Vie," River said. "And you can call the damn sheriff if you want, but I'm looking for Edith."

"Good," Declan said. And it was clear the next admission nearly killed him, but he confessed, "I need your help."

He doubted Declan Sinclair had ever needed anyone or anything.

But Edith did.

If she was missing, something had happened to her. She must be in one of those damn secret rooms. River could find her. He only hoped he wouldn't be too late to help her.

Edith had let another Colton make a fool of her. She'd gone downstairs to investigate, half hoping she would find River looking for whatever the hell he'd been looking for. She hadn't found River, though.

She'd found a woman instead. The blonde had to be in her early fifties, but she looked younger. And maybe that was why Edith had hesitated before using the pepper spray. Maybe it was because she hadn't been able to believe, despite all the pictures she'd seen of her, that this was Livia Colton. Wouldn't she be older? Wouldn't she look mean or dangerous?

Instead she'd smiled warmly. "Edith Beaulieu," she'd said as if she'd been anticipating her arrival. "Mac's little niece grew into a gorgeous young woman."

Maybe the compliment had disarmed Edith. Moments later so had Livia, as she'd swung the handle of a gun. First she'd knocked the canister of pepper spray from Edith's hand. Then she'd knocked her to the ground with a blow to the head.

Edith awakened, she wasn't certain how much later, her head pounding. She was sitting up instead of lying on the concrete where she'd fallen. But when she tried to move, she couldn't. Her arms and legs were bound to the chair in which she sat, a rope wound tightly around her torso, as well—so tightly that she could barely draw a breath.

"Your head must be getting harder," Livia remarked from where she stood next to a control panel of sorts. There were speakers and monitors that displayed rooms in the rest of the house. This must have been where she'd been hiding—the security room. Or a panic room?

Edith was the one panicking, though. She was at the mercy of a woman legendary for being merciless.

"You weren't out nearly as long as the night I knocked those racks over on you," Livia said.

"That was you."

Livia nodded. "Of course. Who else did you think it was?" Her perfect nose wrinkled with disgust. "A *mouse*?"

"Why did you try to hurt me?" Edith asked.

"I wasn't sure what you saw that first night," Livia said. "I was at the bottom of the stairs when you opened the basement door."

Edith shivered as she remembered those eyes glinting in the darkness. She'd convinced herself they'd belonged to an animal. But, given all the horrendous things Livia Colton had done in her life, she *was* an animal.

"I didn't see you," Edith said. At least not well enough to identify what or whom she'd seen.

Livia shrugged, her slender shoulders moving just slightly beneath the silk blouse she wore. For a fugitive, she looked remarkably elegant and rested. "I don't like taking chances."

"Isn't that what you're doing, coming back here?" Edith pointed out.

Livia sighed as if bored with Edith's questions. "There are some chances worth taking."

Was River? Had sleeping with him, falling for him, had he been a chance worth taking? Edith was afraid that she might never have the opportunity to find out— that she might not survive this encounter with Livia Colton.

"Was he helping you?"

"He?" Livia asked as she arched a blond brow.

"River."

For someone who looked so much the lady, with not a dark root showing or blond hair out of place, Livia uttered a surprisingly unladylike snort. "River? That

Boy Scout? You think he would actually help me?" Her
beautiful face twisted into an ugly mask of bitterness.
"You think any of my ungrateful children would help
me? If any of them had known I was here, they would
have turned me in to the authorities immediately."

Her flawless skin flushed with anger. "I gave them
everything money could buy. I made sacrifices to pro-
vide a beautiful home for them, a beautiful life...and I
got nothing in return from them but disappointment."

Edith shivered. She saw now that Livia was a threat
to everyone.

Most especially Edith. She doubted the woman intended to let her go. Now Livia knew for certain that
Edith had seen her.

"All a child really wants is love," Edith said, knowing that was all she'd wanted from her mother—her
love and attention.

Livia looked disgusted. "I thought you were a tough,
practical woman." She shook her head. "You've disappointed me as well, Edith Beaulieu." From that table
with all the monitors, she picked up the gun.

Edith could only hope she'd strike her with it again.
Instead Livia cocked the trigger.

"How?" Edith hastened to ask, stalling for time.
Not that time would help her any. "How did I disap-
point you?"

"You think people need *love*," she said as if she were
using another kind of four-letter word.

But then, Edith had always believed it was a curse,
as well—to love someone. She shook her head. "Not
people, not adults," she said. But she heard the lie in
her voice. "Adults know that love isn't real."

It was real. The love her parents had shared had been

so real. Would River have loved Edith like that had she stopped pushing him away? It didn't matter that she had, though. She'd fallen for him, anyway.

Livia sighed and shook her head. There was no fooling her. "You can stall all you want, Edith. But River isn't going to rush to your rescue like he did all those times before." She gestured toward the speakers on the command table. "I heard your uncle tell you that he was gone. Moving to Austin…" She looked relieved.

While she obviously didn't love her children, maybe she hadn't actually wanted to kill him.

"Did you hit him?" Edith asked, wondering if Livia had hurt him. "With the crowbar?"

"Of course," she said as if it meant nothing to her that she'd given her own child a concussion. "Who else did you think would have?"

"I didn't know if you had help…"

"I told you my children are no help to me at all." She uttered a self-pitying sigh. "They are more a hindrance. A nuisance. A betrayal."

"I meant a man," Edith clarified. "You've been known to use them."

Livia smiled. "Yes, I have. That's another way you've disappointed me, Edith. A woman as beautiful as you are should be using men, not the other way around."

Edith tensed and the ropes tightened around her torso. "You know River was using me."

"I know he was searching for something down here," Livia remarked. "That was why I hit him. I should have killed him…" She clicked her tongue against her teeth, making a *tsk* sound. "And your boss, the new owner of La Bonne Vie, he's been using you, as well."

Now the woman was just trying to upset her. She

was tormenting her. But Edith had to know. "What has River been searching for?"

Livia shrugged. "I don't know for certain—except that it wasn't money. He wouldn't have become a Marine if he were at all interested in money."

A pang struck Edith's heart as she realized how wrong she'd been to accuse River of that. He was no mercenary. He was a hero. "So what was he looking for…?"

"Since weak old Wes Kingston fessed up to not being River's father, I imagine he's been looking for his identity."

"What?" she asked, shocked at the revelation. Claudia had just found out she wasn't a Colton at all. Was anyone whom Edith thought they were? And why hadn't River told her?

Livia stepped closer and pressed the barrel of her gun against Edith's temple. *She* was, unfortunately, everything she was rumored to be—a cold-blooded, psychotic killer.

Edith sucked in a breath as fear overwhelmed her. She tried to wriggle free of her bindings but the restraints were too tight for her to escape. She could only close her eyes as Livia pulled the trigger.

But nothing happened. There was no blast of gunfire. No pain. Just Livia's soft chuckle. "You're not worth the bullet, honey."

Edith gasped at the woman's cruelty and opened her eyes to stare up into the beautiful face of such madness.

"I'll just leave you here to die of dehydration. No one will ever find you."

But Edith could see around Livia's slender frame. One of the monitors showed motion as two men rushed in the front door. Livia turned and saw the monitors and cursed.

"That damn son of mine can't stop playing hero…"

River. River had come to rescue her.

Livia lifted her gun. "Guess I will have to make him stop…permanently."

"No!" Edith shouted.

But it was too late. Livia was already pushing a button that opened the wall onto another room. The one where she'd struck her son. Would she shoot him there, as well?

Fury gripped Livia. She was tired of running. But she found herself rushing along the passageway that would lead out of La Bonne Vie to the acres surrounding it. River had nearly caught her out there one night—when he'd been riding.

But she'd eluded him then, just like she would elude him now. He had found some of the secret rooms but he knew nothing about the tunnels. No one did.

"Stop!" a male voice shouted.

Livia stopped—in shock. She must not have slipped through the door quickly enough. The one leading to the tunnels was at the back of the furnace room. He must have seen her heading to it when he'd opened the basement door.

It wasn't River calling after her, though. But the voice was eerily similar and familiar. She could have started running again, but she was too intrigued. She had to turn back and face the man who'd bought her home. This was the voice she'd heard on the speakers when Edith had talked to her boss—to Declan. And she'd recognized it because he'd sounded so much like her former lawyer.

His appearance jarred her—for just a moment. It was as if she were looking at a ghost. "You look so much like your father," she murmured. Matthew Sinclair had been a handsome man; that was why she'd had to have him. It hadn't mattered to her that he was married.

It had mattered to him, though. He'd had a conscience. That had been a surprise and a disappointment. Lawyers didn't often have consciences, especially the ones who'd worked for her.

"You must be smart like him, too," she mused—to have acquired the wealth it had taken to buy La Bonne Vie.

The son was probably about the age the man had been when she'd seduced him. There would be no seducing Declan Sinclair, though.

He stared at her with hatred hardening his green eyes. There was something else on his handsome face, as well—something very akin to what she'd told Edith she'd been feeling: disappointment.

She chuckled. "Am I not the monster you thought I'd be?" she asked him.

He shook his head. "Not at all," he said. "In fact, you're rather pathetic."

Fury coursed through her. Nobody called Livia Colton pathetic. She raised her gun and squeezed the trigger. Unfortunately for Declan Sinclair, she'd only had one empty chamber.

Chapter 23

The gunshots echoed throughout the basement. River flinched, thinking of them striking Edith. He couldn't tell from where the shots emanated. Declan had headed to one end of the basement by the utility room, while he had headed toward the wine cellar. The shots reverberated, sounding as if they came from every direction.

He flashed back—for just a moment—to all those missions he'd carried out. And to all the casualties he'd carried off the battlefield. He closed his eye. But he didn't see the faces of fallen comrades. He saw Edith's beautiful face, her brown eyes staring lifelessly up at him.

He shuddered and shook off the thought. He wasn't going to lose her. He focused on the gunfire. It almost seemed to be coming from behind the wall of that room where he'd been struck. He'd found one room off that—but that one was empty. He realized now that he'd missed a hidden door. He touched the stone wall and felt it vibrate beneath his hands.

His heart pounded in his chest, it beat so violently. Was Edith being shot to death right now?

Where the hell had Declan gone? Not that River needed his help. He only needed Edith—needed to make sure she was all right. He clawed at the wall until he found the latch and the door propelled open, scraping across the concrete floor.

Edith lay on the floor, slamming the chair to which she was tied against the concrete. She'd broken off a chair leg while scraping up her own skin.

He dropped to the ground next to her and reached out to her with shaking hands. "Are you all right?"

Her hair had tangled around her face. He pushed it off, finding it damp with the tears that streamed from her brown eyes.

"Are you hurt?" he asked her.

She shook her head. "No. I thought—I thought she was shooting you."

"Who?" he asked. But he knew…

The gunfire had stopped, leaving an eerie silence. Edith broke it with the name she uttered. "Livia…"

"She was in here, with you?" That was where he'd heard the shots.

Edith shook her head again.

It was all she could move, River realized. He reached for the ropes binding her. When the knots wouldn't give, he pulled out a pocketknife and used the short blade to saw through them and free her. The skin of her wrists and ankles was raw where the ropes had scraped her. He imagined her stomach was, too, from the rope that had been wound around her and the chair.

He gently moved his fingers across her wrists, trying to restore the circulation in her hands.

Her fingers moved, as she reached up and ran them across his face. "I thought she killed you," she said.

He'd thought the same. That he'd lost her. Knowing that he hadn't, that she was alive, he had to kiss her. He brushed his mouth across hers.

But her lips trembled beneath his and a sob slipped out. "When I knocked my chair over," she said, "I couldn't see the monitors anymore. I could only hear the shots."

River noticed the screens now and the speakers. That was why the shots had sounded as if they were coming from this room. But Edith was alone in it.

"She wasn't shooting at me," he assured her. "I didn't even see her."

"Then who…"

"Me," a deep voice murmured as Declan Sinclair walked into the secret panic room.

Edith jumped to her feet and ran to her boss, throwing her arms around him. River's heart broke at the look of concern on her face.

"Are you all right?" she anxiously asked him.

"Yes," Declan assured her. "She missed…" His brow furrowed as if he wondered how.

River did, too. His mother was a damn good shot. But why would she have spared Declan Sinclair?

"I didn't even know you were here," Edith said.

"She must have," Declan said as he drew back and took in the room they'd found.

River felt sick at the thought of his mother watching him and Edith all this time. But there was no screen in the master bedroom at least.

"I was here earlier but couldn't find you," he said. "So I went over to your uncle's ranch."

River focused on those monitors and noticed movement in one—as a blond-haired woman slipped out of the end of a tunnel. "She's getting away!" When he moved to run after her, Edith caught him.

Her hands grasped his arm. "Don't go," she warned him. "She'll shoot you."

She would kill her son but spare a stranger? River doubted that. Actually, he doubted that Livia would spare anyone. And he doubted Declan Sinclair was a stranger.

"I already called the FBI," Declan told them. "I want her caught, too."

"Why?" River asked.

"She's a fugitive," Declan said as if that answered everything. But it answered nothing at all.

And it was clear from the look on his face that he was keeping a secret. Studying that face again, River suddenly realized why Declan looked so damn familiar to him. His was the face River used to see—before the explosion, before he'd lost his eye.

He'd been tearing the house apart looking for answers, and the secret he'd sought stood right in front of him. "Oh, my God," he murmured. He'd been looking for a father. But he'd found a brother instead.

Edith stared from one man to the other, trying to understand what was happening right before her eyes. River had doubled over as if Declan had struck him. But her boss and foster brother hadn't laid a hand on him.

Declan looked as if he'd been struck, too, even

though he claimed no bullet had hit him. Had he been telling the truth?

"What's wrong?" she asked. She'd been afraid before—when Livia had pressed that barrel to her head and pulled the trigger. But she was nearly as fearful now.

What was happening?

Then she saw it, too—the resemblance she hadn't noticed until now—when they stood nearly side by side. And she shivered as a chill chased down her spine.

Suddenly she knew exactly what River had been looking for in La Bonne Vie. Money had had nothing to do with it. For River...

But now she realized why Declan had been so driven. She understood what he'd wanted with La Bonne Vie, too. And like Livia had said, he'd been using her just like River had. She shivered again.

River straightened up and reached out for her. "You're going into shock, Edith." He glanced at the other man. "Did you call an ambulance, too?"

Declan shook his head. "I didn't know that she'd been hurt. Where are you hurt, Edith?"

Both men seemed full of concern for her. But Edith backed away from them. "Stop!" she shouted. "Stop with your damn secrets. Just admit it."

"What?" They uttered the word in perfect unison. Even their voices were similar.

"You're related."

Declan shook his head. "No, that's not..."

But he didn't finish his denial.

"Clearly it's possible," River said. "How?"

Declan snorted. "How is anything possible with your mother? She seduced my father, like she has so many

other men. He was a smart man—a shrewd lawyer—
and he should have realized he wasn't special to her.
But he thought he was different. Livia made him think
he was different."

And Declan obviously hated her for it.

His voice deepened with resentment and pain when
he continued, "He abandoned my mother and me for
the life he thought he'd have with her. But when Livia
tired of him, as she has every man in her life, he killed
himself."

Edith gasped.

"That's how I wound up in the foster home with
you," Declan told her. "My mother wasn't any more
capable of raising a child alone than yours. She abandoned me on a street corner in New Orleans."

Edith understood his pain. But she was hurting herself. "Was that why you were nice to me?" she asked.
"Because I mentioned the Coltons, that my uncle
couldn't help me because he was too busy with them?"

Declan didn't deny it.

"You used her to get back at us?" River asked. "You
used a little girl?"

"I commiserated with her," Declan said. "I didn't
use her. You're the one who did that."

They had both used her, and Edith had been foolish
enough to let them. She was furious with them but even
angrier with herself. Livia had been right to berate her.

"Neither of you was honest with me," she said, her
voice shaking with her fury.

"Edith—" Again they spoke in unison, then turned
to glare at each other.

Edith had had enough of them. Together, they were
too much for her to handle. Her feelings—of love and

betrayal—overwhelmed her. She couldn't deal with any of it, with them or her feelings.

"Shut up!" she yelled at them both. "It's too late now. You should have been honest with me from the beginning." Because now she would never be able to trust either of them again.

And even worse, she wouldn't be able to trust herself again, either.

"So you want my job?" Jeffries asked as he walked the grounds next to Knox.

Knox turned toward the shorter man. Despite everything he'd done to Knox's family, he almost felt sorry for him. He was in way over his head. "We both know this town has gotten to be more than you can handle."

The FBI was in charge of the search for the fugitive Livia. But they'd been happy to put all available Shadow Creek resources to work searching the acres surrounding the estate. Livia was long gone by now, though.

She had to be. The estate was overrun with authorities searching for her.

Still, Jeffries looked scared. He clutched his weapon tightly while he breathed so hard, his chest nearly popped the already strained buttons on his uniform.

"You think because you were some hotshot Texas Ranger that you can handle this job," Jeffries said resentfully. "But it's tougher than you think—thanks to you Coltons."

Knox didn't doubt that. A hell of a lot had happened recently in Shadow Creek.

"You and this damn town think I can't do my job because I haven't caught her," Bud continued as sweat trickled down his fleshy face. "But your Texas Rangers and the whole freaking FBI can't catch her, either."

Knox had had a text earlier from Joshua Howard. The former Fed had coerced some former colleagues to talk about the investigation. Nobody had a clue where Livia might turn up next, nor did they have a hope in hell of figuring out how to catch her.

They were worried, like Sheriff Jeffries, that she might remain a fugitive forever.

That was why Knox had to run for sheriff. To protect his town and his family from the sociopath that was his mother.

If she was never caught, Livia would pose a constant danger.

Chapter 24

River leaned against the fence of one of the several riding arenas on Jade's ranch, Hill Country Farms. A teenager sat in the saddle on Shadow, nudging him into a gallop around the ring. Despite the kid being the size of a linebacker, tension gripped River as he worried about him and the stallion.

"Are you sure about this?" he anxiously asked Jade.

The horsewoman nodded. "I taught Andy how to ride years ago. He's an excellent rider."

"Andy isn't the problem."

Jade squeezed his arm. "Thanks to you, neither is Shadow."

"Thanks to me?"

"You fixed him, River."

He had been working with the horse for a while. And despite how skittish the stallion had been, it had never thrown him or anyone else. He realized that the horse had never been the danger everyone else had believed him to be.

Relaxing, he chuckled and shook his head. "All I did was ride him." And everyone had thought it was dangerous to risk that. They should have known he'd taken far greater risks than riding a skittish stallion.

He'd fallen for a skittish woman.

"You were patient and kind to him," Jade said. "You made him trust again."

If only he could have accomplished that with the skittish woman…

Instead he had made certain Edith Beaulieu would never trust again. At least not him.

Declan Sinclair would probably have better luck. They had obviously known each other longer—since they were kids.

"You should work here," Jade said. "With me."

He snorted. "I'm not the horse whisperer you are. I'm not even a rancher." He was a Marine. A protector. Being a security guard would give him back the role with which he was most familiar. "I already told Josh I was taking his job."

"But you haven't left Shadow Creek yet," she said.

Maybe he was working on that patient and kind part, hoping that Edith would come around—that she would forgive him. Eventually. It had only been a few days since Livia had captured her and then escaped herself.

Edith wasn't the only one he was waiting to come around, though. He needed to talk to Declan, to find out if Matt Sinclair was really his father, if they were really related…

The enormity of it all had struck him hard that day.

But it had paled in comparison to losing Edith. Would she ever be able to forgive him?

"Josh doesn't have the business quite up and running yet," he explained.

"He and Leonor still arguing over names?"

He grinned. "Probably."

"Is that the only reason you're sticking around?" Jade asked. "Or do you think *she's* still here?"

He actually wasn't sure where Edith was. As furious as she'd been with Declan, she might have quit working for him. Would she have returned to New Orleans?

"I don't know," he replied.

"I think she's still here," Jade said, and her voice cracked with fear.

And he realized she wasn't talking about Edith. "Livia? You think she'd stick around and risk getting caught?" he asked. "Why?"

The color drained from Jade's usually tanned face, leaving it deathly pale. "Because she's going to kill me."

Shock jarred him. "What?"

"That's why she's here," Jade said. "I'm her unfinished business."

"You're not making any sense," he said. "Why would she want to kill you?"

Jade was the baby of the family. Wouldn't even a mother like Livia have a soft spot for her?

"Revenge," Jade murmured.

River took his sister's shoulders in his hands and turned her wholly toward him. He stared down into her face. Her brown eyes were dark with fear and something else. Guilt?

"What are you talking about?" he asked her.

Jade shook her head, making her ponytail swing across the back of her neck.

"Why would she want revenge on you?"

She lowered her voice to a whisper and replied, "Because it was me. I'm the one who helped the FBI take her down."

He nearly laughed. "You were just a kid then," he said. At eighteen he'd still been a child, and Jade was four years younger than him.

"Maybe that was why she underestimated me," Jade said.

River's blood chilled. If his sister was speaking the truth, then there was every chance that Livia would come after her. She would know not to underestimate Jade again.

"What are you talking about?" he asked his sister. "Please tell me…"

She tugged free of his grasp and turned back toward the arena. While she smiled at her riding pupil, the fear hadn't left her eyes. She just shook her head again. "It doesn't matter," she murmured. "What's done is done…"

His sister had secrets that River had never guessed. And not knowing them was frustrating, so frustrating that he understood why Edith was so upset with him and with Declan.

Would she listen if he apologized? Would she forgive if he explained?

Or was it like Jade had just said—*what's done is done*…?

"What's done is done," Declan said as he accepted the resignation letter Edith handed him. "I can't change the past. And what would I have said to you, anyway?"

"The truth," Edith said, her heart still aching with his betrayal. But it wasn't just his that bothered her. His probably didn't even bother the most. But she couldn't work for him anymore. She couldn't be in Shadow Creek anymore, either. She'd packed her bags to leave town, but first she'd tracked down Declan at La Bonne Vie.

She couldn't understand his wanting to be in that house again, where he had nearly been killed. If Livia hadn't missed with all those shots she'd fired...

She shuddered as she thought of how close she'd come to losing him. He'd been such a huge part of her life for so long. So how could he have kept so much from her?

"You were a little girl," Declan reminded her.

"So... I was older than my years, and we both know it," she said. "You could have told me."

"I should have," he admitted. "If not then, then at least when we got older."

She nodded.

And he uttered a heavy sigh. "I can't change the past, Edith. I can't make any excuses, either, but you know how hard it is for me to trust anyone."

"I'm not anyone," she said as tears stung her eyes. "I thought we were family."

"The Coltons are your family, too." And that was why he hadn't been able to trust her.

Had he thought she would say something to one of them? Or had he suspected even then that River was his brother?

"Thorne is the only Colton who's related to me," she pointed out, "and I didn't grow up with him like I grew up with you. You're like my brother."

"And you're like my pain-in-the-ass little sister," he said with a slow grin.

She smiled, too. "I'm only a pain in the ass because I'm always right."

He sighed again. "Yes, you are. Except about this." He crumpled up the letter in his hand. "You can't quit."

She didn't want to. She loved her job—loved the challenge of the empire Declan was building with her help.

"I can't handle any more secrets," she warned him.

"There aren't any," he said. "And there won't be any more."

She nodded. "So you've taken a DNA test, then?"

"What?" He tensed. He knew exactly what she was talking about.

"You and River—you've taken a DNA test to confirm that you are brothers?"

He cursed.

"I'll take back this letter," she offered as she pulled the wadded up paper from his hand, "if you take a DNA test."

"Do you want me to do that for my sake or his?" he asked as he studied her face.

"You just promised there would be no more secrets."

"It's not a secret," he said. "We don't know anything yet."

"You need to know the truth."

"No," he said, and he sounded certain. "I don't need to know the truth."

"River does."

He groaned. "You're in love with him."

She shook her head. "No."

"This complete honesty thing goes both ways," Declan said. "Tell me the truth."

And she groaned now. "It doesn't matter," she said. "I can't trust him."

"No, you can't," Declan agreed. But he didn't sound as certain as he had earlier.

"What?"

He shook his head.

"No more secrets," she reminded him.

"It's not a secret," he said. "It's just an observation. When I told him I couldn't find you in the house, he was really worried about you."

She shrugged. "He's a Marine. It's his thing to protect people." Even his mother had bemoaned the fact that he always had to play the hero.

"It was more than that," Declan said with another heavy sigh. "He was more scared and upset than I was. I think he might love you, too."

Edith's heart swelled and warmed in her chest as hope rushed through it. Was it possible? And would it matter?

If he loved her, maybe she would be able to trust him again. But would she be able to trust herself?

"You don't have to worry that you're like your mother, you know," Declan said.

"What?"

"You're strong as hell," he said. "If you do get sick, you'll find ways to deal with it. You can fall in love."

She snorted. "What do you know about love?"

"We're not talking about me," Declan said. "We're talking about you. I know you. I know you're tough. You're smart. And usually you're brave—except when it comes to relationships. Then you're a damn coward."

"Kettle," she said.

He grinned. "Pot."

He was right, though. She was a coward when it came to love. Too much of a coward to risk her heart—even for River.

Josh gazed around his office with pride. Of course Leonor had done most of the work. She was an amazing decorator. She would be an amazing wife.

Hell, she was amazing at everything she did.

He turned his attention back to the cell phone sitting on his desk.

River's voice emanated from the speaker. "I'm not sure when I can start."

"I thought you were all packed and ready to move to Austin," Josh said.

"That was before we found out Livia had been hiding out at La Bonne Vie."

Josh grimaced as he thought of how close that psychopath had been to his family. And the Coltons were his family now. Not just Leonor's. "That's another reason you should be here."

River snorted. "She's not going to hurt me."

"She hit you with a crowbar."

"And she could have killed me."

But she hadn't.

Josh doubted it was because she'd had an attack of conscience. Livia had proved over and over again that she didn't possess one. River just had a hard head.

"Are you worried about someone else?" Josh asked.

River told him about a conversation he'd had with his younger sister Jade. It wasn't new information to Josh. He knew Livia's case file well.

"You knew," River accused him.

"Yeah…"

"Anything else I should know?" River asked.

"Yeah, who your father is and if you have a brother," Josh said.

River cursed. "I'm not sure I want to work for you anymore."

Josh chuckled. "You know you love me."

He suspected River wasn't hesitating over leaving Shadow Creek because he didn't want to work for him. He had another reason for wanting to stay.

"Who is she?" he asked. Just like he'd known everything else, he knew this, as well. He listened to the family rumor mill.

River wasn't fooled. He cursed him again.

"Talk to her," Josh urged him. "Find out if you have a chance with Edith Beaulieu."

River didn't argue with him this time. He just clicked off the phone, leaving Josh to wonder if his brother-in-law-to-be would take his advice. Or if he'd offered it too late…

Chapter 25

"Thanks for meeting me here," River said as Declan Sinclair walked into Mac's barn. In his suit, he looked out of place among the horse stalls and bales of hay.

He also looked like he wanted to be anyplace else. River suspected that had nothing to do with the barn, though, and everything to do with him.

Declan just gave him a curt nod.

"And thanks for agreeing to the DNA test." It had confirmed what River had suspected and what Declan had obviously already known. They were brothers.

River's last name would have been Sinclair had his father ever known about him and lived to claim him.

"Thank Edith," Declan said. "Agreeing to that test was the only reason she agreed to tear up her resignation letter."

River's heart rate quickened. "She's still working for you?"

Declan nodded. "She still hasn't completely forgiven me for keeping secrets. But we've known each other so long we're like family."

But they weren't.

River and Declan were family, though. River had a lot of siblings. He was used to it. How did Declan feel about it?

"Why didn't you tell her sooner?" River asked.

Declan shrugged. "It doesn't matter anymore."

River snorted. "Yeah, right. You wouldn't have bought La Bonne Vie if it didn't matter anymore. You obviously hate my mother for what she did to your father, to your family." But Matthew Sinclair hadn't been just Declan's father. He was River's, too. "What was he like?"

Declan shrugged again. And River wondered how well the other man remembered him. He couldn't have been very old when he'd died.

"I told you, he was smart," Declan said. "Good-looking. Driven. I can't believe he fell for your mother's manipulations."

"Many men did," River reminded him. "Even Mac…"

"But my dad was savvy," Declan said. "He could always tell when a client was lying. Or when my mother was…" He smiled. "He knew every time she went shopping and spent too much money on shoes."

For as young as he'd been when Matthew Sinclair had died, Declan certainly remembered a lot about him. "He played with me," he continued. "He taught me sports and to read. And…" He released a ragged sigh and shook his head. "It was a waste. Falling for her, killing himself..."

"It was a waste," River agreed, even though had Matthew Sinclair not fallen for her, River wouldn't be here. He wouldn't exist.

Maybe that was why Declan resented him. River understood that reason, and he doubted they would ever have the relationship River had with his other siblings or even that Declan had with Edith.

"I'm not like my mother," River assured him. "I'm nothing like her."

Declan nodded. "I can see that. You're a Marine. You sacrificed for our country. Livia Colton hasn't ever made any sacrifices."

"No, she hasn't," River said. "Is that why you wanted La Bonne Vie—to take away something that mattered to her?" Because her kids damn well hadn't. "She loved that house. That image."

Declan shrugged. "Right now, I don't know what I was thinking."

"What are you going to do with it?" he asked.

Declan shrugged again.

River wasn't certain if the man really didn't know, though. He must have had a plan when he'd bought it. But it was one he didn't want to share. "Has Edith finished the inventory yet?"

"She would have," Declan said, "if you hadn't found those additional rooms. The FBI even discovered a few more when they scanned the entire place. She'll be done soon, though."

"But she's still here?" he asked. "She's still working at La Bonne Vie?"

Declan tensed and hesitated for a long moment before he almost reluctantly replied, "Yes, she's up at the house right now."

"Will you have me arrested for trespassing if I go there to talk to her?" River asked.

"I won't," Declan said. "But I can't promise you she won't. She's still mad at you."

"Then I better watch out for her pepper spray," River said.

And Declan actually chuckled.

It wouldn't be easy, but maybe someday they would be able to have a brotherly relationship.

But that wasn't the relationship River was concerned about at the moment. The one he wanted was with Edith. He could only hope he hadn't blown it.

Edith shouldn't have been nervous about being alone in the house anymore. Sure, she had been through a lot inside the walls of La Bonne Vie. But it wasn't as if Livia could get back inside. It wasn't even as if she were actually alone.

Texas Rangers and FBI agents routinely patrolled the estate, hoping to catch Livia returning. Because of that, there was no way the beautiful fugitive would risk coming back here, though.

Was there?

Livia was crazy, but she was also careful or she would have already been taken back into custody.

No. Edith was safe here now. Finally.

But when she heard the door creak open, fear flashed through her. She fumbled inside her purse and pulled out the canister of pepper spray. This time she wouldn't hesitate to use it.

But before she could press her finger down, she recognized the intruder, as River strode across the foyer to where she worked on boxes Declan had brought up from the basement. Edith hadn't wanted to go down there again.

Ever.

River lifted his hands. "Spray me if you want to," he said. "I know I have it coming."

But did he?

Sure, he hadn't been completely honest with her. But neither had Declan. And she'd forgiven him.

She shook her head. "I wouldn't spray you." She dropped the can back into her purse.

"Then why'd you have it out?" he asked. "I know Declan said you're still mad at him, but…"

"I thought it might be your mother," she admitted. "Though it's ridiculous to think she'd walk right through the front door. I'm overreacting." And she suspected it wasn't the only time she had overreacted.

River sighed. "My mother is capable of anything," he said, "so you're not overreacting at all."

"I'm not?" she asked, as she walked closer to him. Her body ached for his touch. She'd missed him so much, had felt so empty without him.

He shook his head. "Of course not," he said. "Livia had a gun to your head." He shuddered as he recounted the story he must have overheard her telling the FBI agents who'd interrogated her. "I'm sorry for what she put you through."

"It wasn't your fault." She absolved him.

But he still looked guilty, his broad shoulders slumped with the burden of it.

"She's my mother," he said.

"But that doesn't make you responsible for her actions." And as she said it, she realized she wasn't responsible for her mother's issues, either. No matter how hard she'd tried, even if she hadn't been a child, she wouldn't have been able to save Merrilee from her problems.

"I'm responsible for my own actions," he said. "And I'm very sorry that I wasn't completely honest with you from the beginning."

"And I wouldn't have let you anywhere near La Bonne Vie if you had been," she admitted.

He tilted his head and studied her face. "I think you would have. You have a big, kind heart, Edith Beaulieu. You would have understood my wanting to find out who my father is."

Declan had told her the results of the DNA test, which had been no surprise. The men bore such a striking resemblance to each other that they'd had to be related. She didn't know why she hadn't noticed earlier except that, beyond their physical appearance, the men were nothing alike.

"I'm sorry," she said, and she reached out to him, unable to stop herself from offering the comfort she suspected he needed and that she doubted Declan had provided. She linked her fingers with his. "I'm sorry that you found out who he is, only to learn he's already dead."

Linking their fingers, he released a shaky breath. "You can't miss what you never had."

"Is that true?" she asked doubtfully.

"No," he replied. "I miss what we never had. I miss what we could have been together had I been honest with you from the start."

From that amazing night they'd shared, Edith knew

what they could have had. And maybe they could have it yet—if Declan was right and River really had feelings for her.

From the way he looked at her, with such hope and desire, she suspected that he did.

"It was my fault, too," she admitted. "I kept pushing you away."

"I thought that was because you were involved with your boss."

She laughed. "Declan is my brother."

"I know that now."

Her amusement fled. "I was pushing you away because I was scared."

"You?" he scoffed. "Scared? You're the most fearless woman I've ever met."

"I was afraid of falling for you," she said. "I was afraid of falling and then getting sick…the way my mother is."

"You're not your mother any more than I am mine. And if something happens, we'll be okay."

"I know that now," she said. "I'm not afraid anymore."

"Are you still mad at me?" he asked. And finally he touched her. Sliding his fingertips along her jaw, he tipped her face up to his.

"No."

"I'm glad you're forgiving," he said. "Because I'm bound to screw up again."

"Hey!"

"But I love you," he said. "And I will do my best to never, ever hurt you again."

Her breath escaped in a gasp. Then he stole it away

completely as his mouth covered hers. He kissed her deeply—with all the love he'd proclaimed.

She moved her hands over his chest, pushing him back just enough so that she could catch her breath again. His heart pounded fast and hard beneath her palm.

"I'm sorry," he said, "I shouldn't have assumed that just because you've forgiven me—"

"I love you, too," she assured him. "I love you so much." More than she had ever wanted to love anyone. But that overwhelming, all-encompassing emotion didn't scare her anymore. Knowing he loved her just as much made her feel as safe as she'd felt that night she'd slept in his arms with her head on his chest.

With her Marine by her side, she felt invincible.

Hell, she wasn't even afraid of Livia anymore.

Livia Colton had unfinished business in Shadow Creek. She wasn't going anywhere until she settled this score—until she showed exactly what happened to whomever betrayed her. It didn't matter who that person was—friend, foe or child.

She stood outside the gates to Hill Country Farms—just watching and waiting—until the perfect moment to exact her revenge.

She'd had ten years to think about this, to figure out exactly who had betrayed her. And she'd had ten years to plot her revenge. She could wait a little longer to carry out her plan.

* * * * *

MILLS & BOON®

INTRIGUE
Romantic Suspense

A SEDUCTIVE COMBINATION OF DANGER AND DESIRE

A sneak peek at next month's titles...

In stores from 13th July 2017:

- **Dark Horse** – B.J. Daniels *and*
  Cornered in Conard County – Rachel Lee
- **Protection Detail** – Julie Miller *and*
  Secret Agent Surrender – Elizabeth Heiter
- **Manhunt on Mystic Mesa** – Cindi Myers *and*
  Stone Cold Undercover Agent – Nicole Helm

Romantic Suspense

- **Capturing a Colton** – C.J. Miller
- **Cavanaugh Encounter** – Marie Ferrarella

Just can't wait?
Buy our books online before they hit the shops!
www.millsandboon.co.uk

Also available as eBooks.